TAKE BACK THE
BLOCK

TAKE BACK THE
BLOCK

CHRYSTAL D. GILES

Random House 🏠 New York

Copyright © 2021 by Chrystal D. Giles
Jacket art copyright © 2021 by Richie Pope

All rights reserved. Published in the United States by Random House Children's Books, a division of Penguin Random House LLC, New York.

Random House and the colophon are registered trademarks of Penguin Random House LLC.

Visit us on the Web! rhcbooks.com

Educators and librarians, for a variety of teaching tools, visit us at RHTeachersLibrarians.com

Library of Congress Cataloging-in-Publication Data
Name: Giles, Chrystal D., author.
Title: Take back the block / Chrystal D. Giles.
Description: First edition. | New York: Random House, [2021]
Summary: "Sixth-grader Wes Henderson sets out to save the Oaks,
the neighborhood where he's lived his whole life,
from being sold to a real estate developer" —Provided by publisher.
Identifiers: LCCN 2020025245 | ISBN 978-0-593-17517-0 (trade) |
ISBN 978-0-593-17518-7 (lib. bdg.) | ISBN 978-0-593-17519-4 (ebook)
Subjects: CYAC: Community life—Fiction. | Neighborhoods—Fiction. |
Gentrification—Fiction. | Friendship—Fiction. | Middle schools—Fiction. |
Schools—Fiction. | African Americans—Fiction.
Classification: LCC PZ7.1.G5529 Tak 2021 | DDC [Fic]—dc23

Printed in the United States of America
10 9 8 7 6 5 4 3 2 1
First Edition

For my son, Ezra,
may you always take up space,
be visible,
and raise your voice.

1

I spent the morning of my eleventh birthday carrying a sign that read WE WERE HERE FIRST!

There are so many other things I could have been doing on my birthday, but there I was, the only kid, as usual. I had no chance of blending in with the sea of old ladies. Mom didn't like me calling the ladies old, but they *were* old.

I walked a few steps back from everyone, ducking behind my sign as cars sped by. No way was I going to be spotted by some kids from my school. We were out for the summer, but I couldn't be too careful.

It was a thousand degrees outside, and my favorite Carolina Tar Heels blue T-shirt was sticky and clung to my chest. It didn't even match my Nike Air Max anymore. My kicks were now dusty and barely blue. That was my fault, though; I never should have worn my good stuff to trample through dirt.

"Wes, hold the sign up straight and uncover your face," Mom said.

"Come on, Mom, it's hot and I'm thirsty."

"Don't backtalk me!"

I knew better than to talk back, but it was too hot for manners. I wiped the sweat from my forehead and swallowed a glob of spit to wet my throat.

It didn't help.

This was the third march this month, all part of a monthlong protest. The third Saturday I was here instead of playing NBA 2K with Brent and Alyssa. This week's protest was the largest so far. Thirty of us stepped over bricks and construction trash, chanting, "Stop tenant replacement!" Which didn't make much sense, because there were no tenants left to replace.

I got why we were there, but I was a little tired of fighting battles that didn't have anything to do with me, though Mom thinks we belong in the middle of every fight.

This month, we were fighting the development of a new condo building—twenty stories, dark gray tinted glass, space beneath for shops, and even a video game lounge.

I wasn't sure what the big deal was—I thought it sounded pretty cool. The apartment buildings on this street were old and beat-up. New stores would be nice. I didn't say that out loud, though, or I would have had to suffer through at least thirty minutes of enlightenment on history and heritage. Mom always has a speech ready.

Construction on the new building hadn't started yet, but demolition of the old apartment complex had. The tenants had moved out a couple of weeks ago, and now single shoes, stained mattresses, and smashed furniture were the only proof anyone had ever lived here at all.

Just as we rounded the site for the *hundredth* time, I saw a Channel 9 WCTV news van parked on the street in front of the construction site.

"Oh no!" I said under my breath.

A skinny camera operator unloaded a camera and tripod from the van—he set up to film right in the middle of the protest.

Oh shoot! He looked straight at me.

Mom turned and yelled to the group from her spot up front. "This is *our* moment!"

Roars from the crowd got louder. The old ladies started a new chant: *"Whose city? Our city!"*

There was no way I was going to be on the TV news or anywhere near that camera. I'm not exactly the best at speaking in front of people. My mind gets all blurry, and I forget how to talk. I'd be the biggest clown on the block if my friends saw me freeze up on TV again. There was this one time, last year, I was at the Don't Wreck the Rec recreation center cleanup day (boring, I know) and a news anchor asked me why the rec center was important to me. I stood there with a microphone in my face, a cottony mouth, and a fuzzy brain, trying to come up with an answer. Those ten seconds felt like an hour, and I literally came up with zero. It was a complete fail, and since it aired on live TV, I got no do-overs. I wasn't going to let that happen again.

As our group marched toward the news van, I broke away and raced in the opposite direction. I needed somewhere to hide—and quick! I spotted a porta-potty, darted behind it, and dropped to the ground.

As soon as I did, I smelled the funky stench flowing from the poop closet. I inched from behind the potty to find somewhere else to hide—nope, nothing. I was stuck breathing in somebody else's stink juice until the news crew left.

From my hiding spot, I snuck a look at the ladies taking turns speaking into the microphone—they had no problem saying exactly what they meant. This was going to take a while. I passed the time by counting how long I could hold my breath before my lungs started to burn and I had to exhale and inhale again.

After six times, I got up to forty-five seconds before I was gasping for air. When I stuck my head out to get a peek at the news crew again, I saw a second group of protesters starting to arrive across the lot. They were here to trade places with the morning group, which meant Mom and I could leave. Finally! I crawled from behind the porta-potty and rushed past the new group, not even looking back to say goodbye.

A pile of broken concrete blocks was the last thing between our car and me. I leapt on top of it to shorten my path to freedom. I miscalculated my step and stumbled forward into a jagged edge of rock. A strip of blood leaked out of my scratched shin. I kept going.

I turned to see Mom trading hugs with a few of the ladies. "Stay strong!" she called out, her fist raised in the air.

I slumped into the passenger seat and cranked the AC to high as soon as Mom started the car. I hoped she hadn't noticed I'd been MIA when the news crew arrived. Instead, I tried to distract her by using the time on the short drive home to ask about my birthday presents.

"So, Mom, I *have* to have at least one more pair of shoes. I can't start school with last year's shoes."

"Shoes are the last thing you need to be asking for, Wes. There are many more important things in life," Mom said, her eyebrows scrunched and uneven.

That shut me up real quick. Mom always has a way of making me feel guilty about having things other people don't have. I'd rather eat dirt than listen to another lecture on counting blessings. Plus, if we're going

to compare, lots of people have way *more* than I have—
I've seen sneakerheads on YouTube with a whole room
of shoes. I took a deep breath and tried to forget about
the protest.

My breaths got lighter as soon as I saw the rickety
K SINGTON OAKS sign. The E and N were missing, but
I was home. Entering Kensington Oaks is like being
hugged by a grove of oak trees and sunshine. I've lived
in the Oaks my whole life, and I've known all my
neighbors since the days of tricycle races. The houses
and yards are small, but that just means I can hop from
one yard to the next quick enough to make it home
before the streetlights come on.

The Oaks is an inner-city neighborhood—well,
that's what they call it on the evening news. I guess that
means it's a neighborhood full of poor Black people.
To us it's a cocoon in the middle of a crowded city, just
eight blocks from the center of town.

Even though we're surrounded by noise, the Oaks is
calm—quiet, even. That's mostly because of the community's board of organizers. Mom is the board's director. Yep, that means I'm a volunteer, by default.

When Mom pulled into our driveway, I spotted
Mr. Hank waving from his porch across the street.

I hopped out of the car and headed his way.

"Wassup, Mr. Hank?" I said.

"How was the protest this morning? I hate I missed it," Mr. Hank said.

"The same as always. Hot and loud." I knew Mr. Hank would counter with an inspirational quote, but I didn't care. I like Mr. Hank, and his speeches aren't nearly as long as Mom's.

"Wes, you have to look past the physical and see the positive impact," Mr. Hank said.

"Marching in a circle won't stop that building from being built." I shrugged.

Mom walked up before Mr. Hank could give me a piece of his mind.

"Afternoon, Maxine," said Mr. Hank. "Wes was just telling me how great the turnout was."

Mom shot me an evil eye. "Did Wesley tell you he snuck off when Channel 9 showed up?"

I cringed when she called me Wesley. It is my name, but Wes sounds way cooler—it matches my fly.

"He was saying something about that when you walked up," Mr. Hank said. He reached over to give my arm a light pinch.

I smiled to myself. Mr. Hank always finds a way to make me look good in front of my parents, even when I don't deserve it. There was the time I found an old subwoofer in Mr. Hank's trash pile. Me and my friends set it up in the neighborhood park and blasted

J. Cole to crazy levels. When the neighbors complained, Mr. Hank defended me, telling Mom and Dad he'd given me the old speaker to test.

"Let's go, Wes, we have a party to set up for," Mom said.

After all, it was my birthday.

2

I hate having a summer birthday, mostly because I never get to invite all my friends from school to my parties. I *am* lucky to have my crew to hang with all summer long, though: Mya, Brent, Jas, and Alyssa.

The five of us have been best friends since first grade. We all live in the Oaks, except Mya. She and her family moved a couple years ago when her dad got a new job. Now she lives on the Southside—the rich side of town where all the houses are brick and have at least three-car garages. We don't even have one garage, not to mention three. Mya's new house has a pool and a little house near the pool she gets to use for sleepovers. This summer we've taken over Mya's pool at least once a week when we aren't in the Oaks. I think we all secretly wish we had Mya's new life—I know I do.

The whole crew would be coming over for my party later.

When we reached our house, I escaped from Mom and headed straight to the shower. I scrubbed the sweat, dirt, and blood off me and watched it disappear into the drain. I let the water pour over my face until it turned cold. I had to be fresh for my party.

I laid out my favorite Air Max 95s and T-shirt. It had I CONTROL MY ENERGY printed in block letters across the front. I got dressed and headed to the front room.

"Dad, they'll be here soon," I said. "Is the pizza on its way?"

"Chill, son, we have to pick it up. The fancy pizza place you picked doesn't deliver."

"Well, Mya says they have the best pizza in the city."

"Of course she does," Dad said with a smirk.

I waited until we were alone in the car on the way to the pizza shop to ask about skipping the protest next Saturday. If I could get Dad on my side, Mom just might give in.

"Dad, it's important to spend time with your friends, right?" I asked.

"What is it, Wes? No need to sugarcoat it." Dad isn't one for sugarcoating—he'd rather you just spit it out.

"I want to hang out with Brent and Jas next weekend, before school starts. Brent has a new video game we haven't played yet. You know Brent never gets new stuff. Plus, it'll be . . . you know . . . guy time."

Which was only partly true—I *had* played the new game with Brent, but not with Jas.

"Son, you agreed to participate in the march this month. I'd be there too if I didn't have to work. It's the least you can do to help the families that were displaced, like Takari and his family. These are our neighbors." Dad's face was stern—not mad, but serious enough. "Next Saturday will be the last week."

"I know, but it's been three weekends in a row!" I whined. "I'm allowed to have some fun this summer, right?"

Dad gave me a side eye, but after he didn't say anything right away, I could tell he was thinking about it.

"Okay . . . I'll talk to your mom."

"Thanks, Dad. I knew you'd understand," I said, trying to hide a grin.

"Don't push it. And I better not have to utter one word about taking out the trash this week," Dad said, swatting me playfully on the back of the head.

When Dad and I got home, Mom had the house set up for my party. No balloons or anything kiddie this year. We'd start with pizza and wings, watch *Black Panther,* then an NBA 2K tournament. Brent and Jas would sleep over.

"Party people!" Brent yelled when he bounced through the front door.

"Happy birthday, Wes!" Alyssa said with a huge smile, following Brent inside.

Jas walked in next.

"Wassup, Jas! You ready for this tournament?" I asked.

"The question is, are *you* ready?" Jas said, pointing at me.

I laughed. I knew I would crush Jas in NBA 2K. My real competition was Brent and Alyssa. We were the gamers of the crew.

Mya showed up last, as usual. "Let the party begin," she announced as she walked into the kitchen.

When my whole crew was there, Mom and Dad disappeared to their room, leaving us to celebrate.

"What'd you get for your birthday?" Jas asked.

"Nothing yet. My mom always makes me wait until the last minute," I said.

"That's torture. On my birthday, I woke up to pink roses and three new dresses. And that was all the morning of my party," Mya said, pulling out her phone to show us pictures. She was the only one of us with her own cell phone, and every time I saw it, I got a little more jealous.

"Well, we all aren't as privileged as you are, Mya," said Brent, filling his mouth with another bite of pizza. Mya rolled her eyes, but she knew he was right. Even before her dad got his new job, her parents always treated her like a princess.

"I'm sure your parents will get you something awesome, Wes. No worries," Alyssa said.

■ ■ ■

Halfway into *Black Panther,* I had that feeling of being unstoppable. That must be what Mom calls black pride. I've seen the movie like fifty times, but it gets better every time. I imagined myself as powerful and mighty as T'Challa. Jas was Killmonger (a wavy-haired, light brown version), Brent was M'Baku, and Alyssa was definitely Shuri. Mya had named herself designer of the costumes. She wasn't into comics too much, but she loved all the elaborate costumes, and she was always playing around with this design app on her phone. Some of her looks were really good.

Dad came to check on us after the movie was over.

"Everything cool?" he asked.

"Yes sir," we all said at the same time.

"Hey, Wes, come here," Dad said, motioning me over to the kitchen. "Quick question: Did you invite Takari?"

"Well . . . no. I wanted to, but he and Mya don't get along," I whispered.

"Son." Dad's voice was low.

"I know," I said, looking down at the floor. "Dad, can we talk about it later?"

"We definitely will," Dad said, then turned to walk away.

I tried to brush off the look of disappointment in Dad's eyes before I rejoined the group.

"Was that about Kari?" Jas asked.

"Yeah," I said.

"Thanks for not inviting Takari Brown the Weirdo," Mya said.

"Mya, that's not fair. He and his family have been through a lot," said Alyssa.

"Yeah, whatever," Mya said.

"Look, it's my birthday," I said. "I don't want to talk about Kari. Let's get this tournament started!"

Brent and Mya were up first.

"You ready for this beatdown?" Brent said. He put on a fake grimace and stood over Mya.

"Back up," she said, pushing him out of her face. "I don't even know how to play, but since it's Wes's birthday, I'll pretend to be interested."

"Finally, something you aren't good at," Brent said.

Brent got an early lead. Mya broke down and gave up in the third quarter.

Next were Jas and Alyssa. No junk-talking this round. Alyssa could have put up a hundred points on Jas, but she took it easy on him. She only beat him 85 to 60.

The winners of those rounds had to play each other. Alyssa and Brent grabbed the controllers and got ready to battle.

"I'm not playing nice," Brent said. "Get ready to go down."

Alyssa smirked. She gave Brent a nice, quiet beat-down. No bragging needed.

Since it was my birthday, I played the winner of the last round. I was ready—I love coming up with a winning strategy and then the rush of controlling every play. My heart pounded a little when I took Brent's seat. I usually beat Brent by talking enough smack to get him off his game. That wouldn't work with Alyssa; she was a quiet killer. We grabbed the controllers and got to work.

By the end of the third quarter, there had been six lead changes and I was up by four points.

"You got her, Wes!" Jas yelled from the sidelines.

Alyssa just kept playing. Right when I thought I would take it, she started raining threes. In no time, she was up by six.

With one minute left in the fourth quarter, Alyssa pulled ahead by nine and I knew it was over. I sat stunned and watched the game clock tick to :00.

An *L* on my birthday? I would never live this down.

3

In the morning, after the best birthday sleepover—with almost no sleep—Jas pumped music into his earbuds while Brent and I played Racers. It's a preowned no-name car-racing video game, my birthday present from Brent. After the game glitched for the fourth time, I was over it.

"Man, where'd you get this game from?" I asked Brent as I tossed my controller on the bed.

"Come on, let's try it one more time," he said, ignoring my question. "You gotta admit the graphics are nice, and look at all the cool places we've raced."

Brent did have a point; we'd raced through cities all over the world—across bridges and through beaches—and it did make me feel like I was in another place.

That's one of the things I like most about Brent—his way of turning something so-so into something good. Maybe that's why Brent's my best friend. Not that I'm not tight with the rest of the crew, but he's my *best* best friend. There was the time in fourth grade when Brent and I were paired for a project in art class. We had to make a collage of our favorite vacation memories. The only problem was that neither of us had ever been on a real vacation. I was too embarrassed to admit that to Ms. Bradley, and I definitely didn't want the other kids to know.

Brent came up with the idea of making a collage of all the cool places our favorite rappers talked about: Saint-Tropez, Miami Beach, Santorini, New York City, and the Hollywood Hills. We clipped pictures from magazines of all the luxurious places and pasted our favorite lyrics under the images. We had the most interesting collage in the whole class.

I was sure someone would pick at us for cheating and choosing places we had never visited, but no one cared that we'd never seen any of the places in real life.

After we were both over the racing game, Brent, Jas, and I left my house and headed to the community park at the end of my block. We shot hoops for a while at the court, then walked a couple blocks over to Central Community Church.

On Sundays, when the church dismisses, some of the younger drummers from the band stay around to put on a show on the church's front lawn. Even though we don't go to the service, we like to listen to the drummers do their thing. Bunches of people hang around to dance and talk and drop a few coins in a bucket as a thank-you for the dope beats.

"Man, it's hot as fire out here," Brent said. "Y'all really want to stand outside listening to some drums?"

It *was* hot—hot as fire, even, but the drummers were worth a little sweat.

"Come on, Brent. It's summer. . . . It's supposed to be hot," Jas said. "Plus, I've been practicing a new beat. I almost have it down." Jas whipped his drumsticks out of their permanent spot in his back pocket and air-tapped a beat.

Of the three of us, Jas is the musical one. He's been playing the drums since I've known him. His mom says he was born with music in his fingers and toes. I think he would give up everything else if he could play drums and listen to music all day, every day. He likes to join the drumline on Sundays, and sometimes they even split the change with him.

"If you make some money today, you owe me half," Brent said. "Deal?"

"No deal," Jas said, poking Brent with one of his drumsticks.

Brent and I blended into the crowd while Jas went to help the drummers set up. They kept it old school by banging on buckets while they stood up or sat on crates.

After one of the other drummers intro'd the set, Jas chimed in with his newly practiced beat. It was good—and got the crowd rocking and dropping coins into the bucket. It was a full-on party when the other drummers joined in. Hands were clapping, feet were gliding, and sweat was pouring. Even Brent stopped complaining and got into it.

Random people walking down the street stopped to watch and listen. The group had grown large enough to spill out onto the curb when I spotted Kari. It was only the second time I'd seen him all summer, which was kinda weird, since I was used to having him at my house all the time. His mom and my mom have known each other since forever.

Kari lived in Kensington Oaks until a few years ago—back when he was part of the crew. Not that he isn't now, but when his parents split up, his dad moved away, and his mom, Ms. Tasha, moved Kari and his sister to an apartment downtown, so he isn't around much. Last month, they had to move out of the apartment because of the new condo building construction. Which sucked for Kari. He deserved to be somewhere nicer. The protest marches were for his family and others like them.

I left Brent to join Kari near the curb. "Where've you been, Kari?" I shouted over the drums.

"Hey, Wes," Kari said. "I've been around."

"Ummm, okay," I said. "Just haven't seen you . . ."

"Your birthday was yesterday, right?" Kari said, changing the subject. "Happy birthday. I bet you had fun."

"Ummm, yeah, it was okay. Just had a couple people

over. I wanted to invite you, but I don't have your mom's new number and—"

"It's cool," Kari interrupted.

I swayed from one foot to the other. I miss Kari, and I hate leaving him out of stuff, but the truth is, I don't know how to be his friend anymore. I'm not sure where he lives. After the apartment building was torn down, Kari and his family had to leave, but no one knows where they went, and Kari can be weird about sharing personal stuff. Plus, he and Mya aren't really feeling each other, and since Alyssa and Mya are super tight, things can get messy fast.

"Maybe we can hang out sometime. Just me and you. Like old times," I suggested.

"That would be cool."

"Tomorrow? My house? I mean, if you can."

"Yeah, I can," Kari said.

■ ■ ■

I hoped Kari would really show up. I spent the evening cleaning my room just in case. I rearranged my sneaker collection to display the newest pairs on the wall across from my bed, and I moved the older pairs into the closet. The room is small, but I take advantage of every inch of space.

My bed is just two steps from the door; if I roll too far, I end up in the hallway. Yep, that's happened. The wall behind the bed is reserved for my puzzles. They're kinda my thing. I started collecting them a few years back when Mr. Hank gave me one for my birthday. He said I needed something to stimulate my mind and video games didn't count. I spent hours piecing together that first puzzle, and even though I never told him, Mr. Hank was right. I was hooked—something about taking a broken picture and slowly clicking each piece into place, making it whole again, made me feel good. When I was done, I wrapped it in special stick-n-peel plastic and hung it up. Now I have a collection big enough to cover half the wall. My latest is a still of Stephen Curry's overtime three-pointer to beat the Oklahoma City Thunder. Steph's my man; he has the smoothest three-pointer in the game.

The only thing as precious as my wall of puzzles is my wall of sneakers. I have it set up similar to a shoe store, with two rows of boxes lined up against the wall. I can show off ten pairs without Mom freaking out on me. I've even worked out an exchange deal with a few other kids in the neighborhood. When it's time for me to size up, I have a new supply waiting on me.

■ ■ ■

Ding dong!

The next afternoon, Mom ushered Kari inside and handed him a glass of water. "Honey, you're dripping wet. Let's get you under the AC."

"Thanks," Kari mumbled, his eyes low.

"Kari! You played a game of HORSE on the way here?"

"Nah, man, it's just a little hot outside," Kari said between gulps of water. *More than a little hot.* His shirt was three shades darker around the neck and chest and under his armpits.

"Well, come on—let's go to my room and get on this Fortnite."

"Wes, give Kari a clean shirt," Mom said. "Kari, you're at home. Need anything, just ask."

"Yes ma'am," Kari said.

While Kari changed his shirt, I wondered where he'd come from. He must've walked a long way. I didn't ask, though. He hadn't been around in a while, and I didn't want to mess it up.

Kari's eighteen months older than me, but we've always been close—until recently. When Kari and his family lived in the Oaks, we slept at each other's house every weekend. And even though Kari didn't always get along with the other kids in the neighborhood, I didn't mind. Ms. Tasha called him eclectic. "He dances to his own drumbeat," she always said. I figured Kari is just Kari.

He isn't into sneakers or sports, and he always wears his hair in a new style. Just last year, he rocked four different hairstyles. Bald fade, low fade, baby Afro, then twists. This year he started growing locs. They were short, frizzy, and uneven—kinda like him. Today he was dressed in cutoff shorts and a faded pink T-shirt.

I peeked at the strings hanging from his shorts. I wouldn't be caught dead in that outfit. I like a clean look. I have the best edge-up on the block, and I pride myself on being named Best Dressed in fifth grade, a title I expect to carry into sixth grade.

"You still hang with Brent and Jas?" Kari asked.

"Yeah," I answered, hoping Kari wouldn't bring up my birthday party again.

"How's Mya? I bet she doesn't step foot in the Oaks anymore," Kari said with a slight grin.

"She came over for my . . . uhhh . . . birthday. But yeah, you're right. She hardly comes around anymore," I said. Mya makes her own schedule and always has some cool things she's doing—dance class, art class. She even has a book club. She's basically a grown woman in an eleven-year-old's body.

After an awkward silence, I blurted out, "Look, Kari . . . I'm sorry I haven't invited you over lately. I didn't know you were going to get kicked out of your place. Mom said you guys only knew two weeks before you had to be out."

"It's cool, Wes."

I could tell Kari was mad, though. I'd picked Mya's pool party over helping him move this last time. Which sounded really messed up, but I had promised Mya, and the rest of the crew was there. Mom said I needed to make things right, but I didn't know how. It wasn't my fault Kari's parents got divorced and he had to move. And it wasn't my fault things were all weird with him and Mya.

"No, for real, I wanted to help you pack your stuff up . . . but Mya had a pool party on the same day."

"Look, me and my family aren't your responsibility," Kari said. "We have enough pity. We don't need yours too."

Flames came off Kari's words. "That's not what I meant," I said.

This is exactly why I hadn't invited him over lately. I barely know what to say to him anymore, especially now. It's like walking on stilts—one false move and *bam!*

"Let's just play the game," Kari said. "You're my little bro. It's no biggie."

Kari and I spent the next three hours battling on Fortnite. There wasn't much talking, but after a few minutes we got into the game and it was almost like old times, like our argument hadn't even happened.

"You ready for school to start next week?" I asked.

"Not really," Kari answered.

"I'm in Mr. Baker's homeroom. I heard he's tough."

"I had him for homeroom in sixth grade too. He's not that bad. You nervous to start middle school?"

Brent, Jas, Alyssa, and I would all be starting at Oak Grove Middle. It's the neighborhood middle school, across the street from Oak Gardens Elementary. Mya also convinced her parents to drive her from the Southside so we could all stay together. Her dad agreed to a two-month trial at the Grove, whatever that means, but Mya pretty much gets anything she asks for, and we've always gone to the same school.

"Everybody keeps asking me that. Not really. All my friends will be at the Grove too, so I don't think it'll be that different. Plus, you'll be there, right?"

Kari looked away. "Yeah, I'll be there," he said finally.

"Who do you have for seventh-grade homeroom?" I asked.

"I'm not sure yet. My papers got lost in the mail. Ya know, during the move," Kari said.

I wasn't sure what to say, so I nodded and kept playing the game.

It was almost dinnertime when we wandered to the kitchen for a snack. Dad was just coming in from work at the car dealership. He unbuttoned his oil-stained uniform shirt and tossed it on the couch.

"Walter, get that dirty shirt off my couch!" Mom yelled over her shoulder.

Dad laughed and picked up the shirt and threw it in the basket beside the washing machine. That routine replays itself every day, and it never gets old.

"Hey, son," Dad said. "Kari, we've missed you around here."

"Hi, Mr. Walter."

"You guys ready for dinner?" Mom asked.

"Yes ma'am," I answered for both of us.

Mom had made Kari's favorite meal. Meat loaf, garlic mashed potatoes, green beans, homemade biscuits, and peach sweet tea. She's the best cook—like chef level— and she outdoes herself when we have guests over.

"Wes, bless the table," Mom said once we were all sitting down.

"Dear Lord, thank you for this food. Thank you for this day and thank you for Kari. Amen." Mom flashed me a quick grin. I knew she was happy me and Kari had made up.

I liked when we had a fourth person at the table for dinner. Being an only child means I'm always the only one being asked questions. Today was Kari's turn. Besides, maybe Mom and Dad could get Kari to spill where he and his family had moved to.

"Kari, did y'all get settled into your new place yet?" Mom asked.

"I guess so. I lost a lot of my stuff, though."

"Stuff like what?" Mom asked.

Kari shifted in his chair and finally whispered, "Clothes and stuff."

That's why he was wearing those busted shorts.

"Well, you know, A Place Called Home is sponsoring a clothing drive in a couple weeks. You be sure to come down and get some clothes. Wes will be there too, helping out," Mom said.

"Yes ma'am," Kari said.

Dinner went along just like that, Mom asking questions and Kari answering with as few words as possible. But Kari must have really enjoyed the food, because he left his plate spotless *and* he volunteered to clean the kitchen.

Of course, that meant I had to help.

I glared at the mountain of dirty dishes. White, slimy potatoes stuck to the bottom of the pot were my worst nightmare. I leaned over to Kari and whispered, "Man, we could be finishing our game. It's not even my night to do the dishes."

"Come on, it won't take long," Kari said, nudging me.

"Wes, are you complaining about cleaning? There is a certain thing next Saturday," Dad reminded me.

"No sir!" I answered quickly. I'd rather do dishes every night this week than march next Saturday—well, maybe not every night.

Kari grabbed the sponge and got to work scrubbing the food-crusted pots while I washed the plates and cups. Kari didn't try to get away with soaking the pots overnight like I did. He took his time and scrubbed each pot clean. We have a perfectly good dishwasher, but Mom always says, "No need to use a dishwasher when you have two good hands."

After way longer than it should have taken, the kitchen was finally clean. Kari did most of the work, so I guess it wasn't too bad, except for my wrinkled fingertips and bubble-soaked shirt.

"It's getting late. We need to get you home," Dad said to Kari.

"That's okay, Mr. Walter, I can walk." Kari looked down at his feet.

"Not up for discussion. We'll all go." Dad grabbed his keys and headed for the front door.

Mom sat up front with Dad, and Kari and I climbed into the back seat of our SUV. Kari and I were sitting next to each other, but something felt different— we were suddenly miles apart again. The bond we'd built over video games and dirty dishes had disappeared. Kari sat quietly staring out the window, his face blank.

He had crawled back into his shell. He'd changed so much. I wished we could turn back and go home.

"Downtown, right?" Dad guessed.

"Yes sir. Left on Third, then a right on Martin Luther King Jr. Boulevard," Kari instructed.

The knot in my stomach got bigger with every turn. I wasn't sure where we were going, but this wasn't a part of town I went to often.

"Left here," Kari said. "Okay, this is it."

Dad rolled the car to a slow stop behind what looked like a small hotel. There were chairs and tables set up outside on the grass. A group of kids chased each other across an open lot. We'd gone just a few blocks, but it felt so far from Kensington Oaks.

Two men who were sitting in chairs and playing cards looked over at our SUV like we didn't belong there.

"Come on, Kari, I'll walk you to the door," Dad said.

Dad and Kari disappeared into a covered walkway that led to the bottom level of the hotel.

The minutes oozed by while we waited for Dad to come back. I watched the kids playing outside and wondered if these were Kari's new friends.

Boom!

I jumped and turned to see that a brown glass bottle had hit the ground and shattered into a million pieces.

The foamy liquid inside spilled onto the ground. One of the cardplayers stood up, shouting and pointing at the other guy. Then, just as quickly as he'd stood up, he sat back down and dealt another hand.

When Dad returned to the car, no one said a word. The drive home felt like the longest round of the quiet game.

I sat in the back seat thinking about how strange it would be to live in a hotel. The only time I even stayed in a hotel was when we visited family up north, and even then it was only for a couple days. I don't blame Kari for not wanting to tell us.

When we pulled back into our driveway, Dad turned to me. "What you saw tonight stays between us. It's no one else's business."

"Yes sir" was all I could mumble.

4

The first day of middle school is a big deal. It's an even bigger deal for the Best Dressed titleholder, which happened to be me. There are certain times you should come to school with the freshest look possible: the first day of school, the day after Christmas break, and the day after spring break. I'd picked out my outfit weeks ago: indigo denim shorts and a royal-blue Supreme T-shirt. Until yesterday, the only things missing were the new Steph Currys that Mom had surprised me with as a late birthday present.

With one last stroke of the hairbrush, my waves floated right up to the shore of my crispy edge-up. I rubbed on one more coat of lotion, dashed out the door, and headed to school.

I met up with the crew in the courtyard of the Grove. The courtyard was in the middle of all the action—a gathering spot where the kids hung out talking and chillin' before class—the perfect spot to get your brand-new outfit noticed.

I was happy to see everyone looking good for the first day of sixth grade. Brent had gotten the top of his fade dyed red, Jas's faux-hawk was neatly trimmed, and Alyssa rocked some new braids. Alyssa always wore her hair in braids, sometimes up, sometimes down, and sometimes two cornrows straight back. I knew Mya would have a dope new hairstyle too.

"Your mom let you dye it?" I asked Brent, pointing at his hair.

"Let me?" Brent asked. "I'm my own man . . . but yeah, she let me." We all laughed 'cause we knew Brent had to do some serious begging to get Mrs. Williams to say yes.

I was glad she did, though, 'cause Brent hardly ever gets new clothes, and he does what he can to stay fresh.

We watched the other kids strut by in their new outfits. Yeah, some of the older kids looked good, but I had no competition with the kids in my grade. I had the first-day-of-school swag in the bag.

I know looking good isn't everything, but it's one of the best things. Dad always says, "Style is a language." I get my style from Dad. I'm a mini-version of him. We have the same medium-brown skin and lanky build, and he tries to keep up with my shoe game.

The opening bell blared through the speakers, signaling the start of homeroom.

"Ready?" I asked Brent, Jas, and Alyssa.

"Let's go," Brent said.

If he had any first-day-of-middle-school jitters, I

couldn't tell. Jas, on the other hand, had barely said a word since we got there. He'd had his earbuds in all morning, which was normal for Jas. He doesn't go anywhere without a pair of earbuds. He says they only let in the sounds he wants to hear. Plus, I think he was a little nervous about meeting new people.

Us boys led the way to homeroom while Alyssa dragged behind.

We headed across the courtyard and down a long hallway toward a two-story brick building. This place was like three times the size of Oak Gardens. Alyssa and I turned left at the end of the hall, while Brent and Jas took a right. They were both in Ms. Marquete's homeroom. She was supposed to be a lot nicer than Mr. Baker.

Alyssa was several steps behind me.

"You okay?" I asked, stopping so she could catch up.

"Have you heard Mr. Baker is kinda mean?" Alyssa was giving me scared vibes.

"Kari said he's not that bad. Mya will be with us too. You'll be fine. Come on, the warning bell's ringing."

"When did you talk to Kari?" Alyssa asked.

"He came over last week," I said.

"How is he? He's still in school here, right?"

"He said he was." Honestly, I wasn't sure. I hadn't seen or talked to Kari since we dropped him off at the hotel. I was a little nervous to see him today. I wasn't sure what he'd say about it. I wished I could tell Alyssa, but like Dad said, it was nobody else's business.

Mr. Baker stood in the doorway welcoming each student into the class. He was even taller than I'd heard. He towered over us as we walked through the door. His outfit wasn't half bad, though, navy-blue pants and a white dress shirt that had his initials stitched on the left wrist cuff. Brown leather suspenders held up his pants, and he sported a striped bow tie. Word is he used to be a lawyer, and he definitely dressed like it.

"Sit wherever you'd like. I will only assign seats if you prove to me that you can't handle choosing your own seat," Mr. Baker said. His booming voice echoed off the walls.

Mr. Baker also taught sixth-grade social studies. Maps and posters of kids from all over the world covered the walls of his classroom. The desks were set up in four rows. Alyssa and me grabbed two seats next to each other on the second row and saved a seat for Mya. Homeroom sped by with only enough time for Mr. Baker to review his class roster, tell us where our lockers would be, and help a couple kids with their class schedules.

Mya showed up right before homeroom was dismissed. Her special entrance included a whole speech about the "insane traffic from the Southside." Mr. Baker didn't seem happy at all about Mya being late, and he seemed even more irritated about her traffic speech.

"Ms. Cooper, please have a seat," he said in his boomy voice.

Mya wasn't off to a good start with Mr. Baker, and I kinda felt bad for her. I waved her over to our row, and she squeezed in beside Alyssa.

Instead of walking us to our lockers, Mr. Baker gave us a diagram with a bunch of squares and our last names written inside a square. According to the boxes, my locker was on the same row as Mya's and Alyssa's— not sure how we got that lucky.

Our schedules were broken out into blocks, which were just long classes—me and Alyssa had two blocks together, math in the morning and social studies in the afternoon. That made me happy. At least I'd have a built-in math tutor; Alyssa was a whiz in math.

By the end of first block, I knew I'd definitely have to lean on her a little, because after getting two math homework assignments on the first day, I felt like I was already behind.

Ms. Hardy, the math teacher, was possibly meaner than Mr. Baker was, and no one even warned me. She had us line up on one side of the classroom, and we had to answer a question before we could sit down. Mine was, how many cups are in a quart? The bad news is I got the answer wrong (there are four cups in a quart, not six). The good news is my seat was directly behind Alyssa and directly beside a boy named Lawrence from my fifth-grade class.

After first block, Alyssa, Mya, and I met Brent and Jas in the café for lunch. The café was a regular school cafeteria, but bigger and fancier. The rumor was, a few years back there was a rat infestation in the old cafeteria, shutting it down for a whole week. A sponsor donated some money to the school to fix the rat problem and get better food. Now we had real fruit and vegetables—not the stinky canned ones—and meat-free and nut-free items. I wasn't sure about the rat story, but I was happy that we could pick our own seats, and the food didn't sound bad.

I scanned the huge café for Kari. No sign of him anywhere, and with how big the place was, I'm not sure I would have seen him anyway.

Mya and Alyssa went to find a table while Brent, Jas, and I filed into the lunch line. Mya wouldn't be caught dead eating school food. I think Alyssa only brought her lunch so Mya wouldn't feel left out. Alyssa usually does whatever she can to make Mya happy. They were cousins—well, fake cousins, which really meant best friends.

"Hey, is that Kari?" asked Jas, popping out his earbuds and pointing across the room.

"Yeah, it is," I said.

Jas waved his arms in the air to get Kari's attention.

"Hey, Kari!" Jas said when Kari walked over to join us in the lunch line.

"Jas, wassup?" Kari was wearing the same cutoff shorts he wore last week, a plain white tee, and some Vans that actually looked new.

"Nothing. How was your summer? You moved, right?" Jas asked.

"It was okay," Kari said, ignoring the question about him moving.

I stood motionless, waiting on Kari to acknowledge me.

"Hey, Wes. Mr. Baker wasn't too bad, was he?" Kari asked.

"No, he was okay." I took a deep breath and tried to be cool. Maybe things between us were back to normal after all.

"Want us to save you a seat?" Brent asked Kari.

Kari looked over at Mya and Alyssa sitting at a table across the lunchroom. "Nah, that's okay." He knew what I knew; things were easier when he and Mya weren't around each other.

Kari disappeared across the café, and Jas, Brent, and I moved through the lunch line.

Instead of square, soggy pizza and tough, over-salted corn kernels like we were forced to eat at Oak

Gardens, there were little stations set up where you could choose the food you wanted. Today there was a mashed potato bar, turkey pot roast, grilled chicken, and a fruit-and-vegetable bar. The grumbling in my stomach meant I was impressed.

"I'm about to grub!" Brent said, jumping in front of Jas.

"You always grub. You're first in line whenever you smell food," Jas said.

"I gotta feed these muscles," Brent said, flexing his biceps at Jas. "You need to get like me."

Jas just laughed. Winning a word battle with Brent was impossible; any battle, for that matter. They were exact opposites. Brent stood several inches taller than Jas and even taller if he stood on his confidence. Jas was Mr. Zen. He probably listened to drumbeats, chirping crickets, or spring rains in those earbuds. We filed through the line and met up with Alyssa and Mya at the table.

The rest of the day went smooth. So did the rest of the week, just like I'd thought.

Except for math class.

No matter the school or the teacher, math isn't my thing. I had a feeling Ms. Hardy and me weren't going to get along. She was one of those teachers who called on you even when your hand wasn't raised. But

Mr. Baker was all right—he actually reminded me of a white version of my dad. He meant business, but he had a funny joke every now and then. I'd also decided, after a week of fresh outfits, that Mr. Baker was the best-dressed teacher at the Grove.

···

On Saturday, I woke up to Lauryn Hill's voice floating through the house. Lauryn was singing about "that thing"—which meant Mom was up early cleaning. When there aren't any protests, Saturday mornings are for R&B and housework. I secretly like when Mom plays old-school music; she'll dance around the house while Dad watches her sway to the beat. She acts like she doesn't notice him watching her, but she'll glance over her shoulder every few minutes to catch him staring. They can be so corny sometimes.

Mom and Dad met when they were in high school. Mom said Dad was afraid to make the first move because she was taller than him. Dad got over the height thing and asked her on a date, and the rest was peaches and cream. (Dad's words, not mine.) Nowadays the height thing isn't a big deal, unless Mom styles her puffy curls into an Afro, adding several inches Dad can't compete with.

I'd spent the night before sorting out what clothes I would donate to the clothing drive. I'd packed two full boxes of shirts, jeans, and jackets. I had a few pairs of sneakers that were too small, but I wasn't ready to part with them just yet.

"Wes! Brent and Jas are here!" Mom called.

I'd convinced them to join me. Brent and Jas are pretty cool about helping with my volunteer chores, except for marching—they wouldn't be caught anywhere near a protest march. Honestly, I think they feel sorry for me.

"My guys. Wassup?" I said when I met them at the door.

"Hey, Wes, let me grab those boxes. You look like you're about to fall over," Brent said, punching my arm.

"They're all yours," I said, and placed the boxes at his feet.

"Let's go, boys. I'll drop you off at the shelter and be back to pick you up around four o'clock," Dad said.

I was happy not to have my parents tag along. Ms. Grave runs the clothing drives at A Place Called Home, the shelter a few blocks over. She's a short, fun lady with frizzy hair and everybody likes her. She lets us play music, and we usually get to pick what jobs we do. Mom and Dad would be collecting donations from people around the city while us kids worked the clothing drive—which was fine with me.

I'd asked Alyssa to meet us at the shelter too. Alyssa doesn't mind helping with my volunteer stuff either. Her mom is also on the community board. Alyssa isn't forced to be at all the events I get dragged to, but she's at enough to make me stand out less. At the last clothing drive this past spring, me and Alyssa were the only kids sorting clothes and unpacking boxes until after dark on a Saturday night. I guess we have more in common than I ever knew, or maybe I just wasn't paying attention before.

When we reached the shelter, we saw Alyssa and Mya standing on the curb.

"What's Mya doing here?" I said.

We unloaded the boxes from the trunk and headed over to the curb to meet them.

"Mya, I'm surprised to see you here. This isn't your kind of thing," Jas said.

"I asked her to come," Alyssa said. "She's staying at my house tonight."

"Let's check in with Ms. Grave. She'll tell us what she wants us to do," I said.

Ms. Grave let everyone pick their assignments. Jas and Brent would unload boxes from cars dropping off donations. Alyssa and Mya would sort the items, and I would escort the patrons to the correct line. I was hoping to get paired with Alyssa, but now that Mya was here, I should have known they'd be stuck together like glue.

Not even an hour into the clothing drive, I spotted Kari walking up to the shelter. *Oh no!* I had forgotten Mom told him to come. I ran over to stop him from getting in line.

"You didn't tell me everybody would be here!" Kari said when he saw me.

Before I could even respond, the rest of the group came over to say hello. *This is all my fault.* I should have remembered Kari would be there; he'd never feel comfortable getting free clothes now.

"Kari, I'm glad you could make it," I said. "You can help me escort people through the line. I'll go tell Ms. Grave you're here."

"Okay, cool," Kari said, going along with me.

When everyone except Mya came over to talk to Kari, he walked up to her to say hi.

"Wassup, Mya?"

"Takari."

Mya didn't even look up. She'd been giving Kari an attitude ever since that incident at her birthday party.

Mya is known for having epic birthday parties. She plans exactly how she wants things to be. When she turned ten, she had everyone dress up in their dopest outfit and walk down a runway for her fashion show. She had judges and everything. I won first place, and my prize was a hundred-dollar gift card.

This year she had a carnival-themed party, complete

with costumes and a photo booth. Mya was the carnival princess. She took pictures with everyone in the photo booth. When it was Mya and Kari's turn, they made funny faces and used all the best props. For the last shot, Kari and Mya both made kissy lips, looking into the camera. I didn't think it was a big deal, but when the machine spat out the pictures, the rumors started.

Everyone sang, "Mya and Kari, sitting in a tree, *k-i-s-s-i-n-g* . . ." and "Mya loves Kari . . ." Then Brent gave them the couple name Ka'Mya, which sent Mya over the edge. Her face went from pink to red to redder the more we laughed. And when I called Kari *Mari* by mistake, Mya lost it.

She blamed Kari for not squashing the rumor. She blamed Kari for laughing. She even blamed Kari for coming into the booth with her.

Kari apologized at least one hundred times, but it was too late—Mya has never forgiven him and probably never will. Which isn't fair, but I don't know how to fix it, and I'm not about to be uninvited to Mya's parties because of some beef with her and Kari, especially since half the time he isn't around anyway.

Since then, the crew's been divided—an incomplete puzzle.

If Kari's around, Mya doesn't want to hang out . . . and Alyssa doesn't want to be here if Mya's not here.

Which is weird because Alyssa lives on my street—plus, her mom and my mom are really good friends. Honestly, things are a lot easier when Kari's not around.

I know Kari would take that moment back if he could, and it really wasn't his fault. I also know Kari has a secret crush on Mya. A crush he might as well forget about. She has no interest in him—or any other boy, for that matter. If it doesn't involve fashion, hair, or glam, it doesn't interest Mya. She's already made up her mind to be a famous fashion designer. She'll move to New York City, go to Parsons School of Design, and be rich by the time she's twenty-five.

So, with all the drama between Mya and Kari, he stayed by me during the clothing drive, helping out where he could. Alyssa and I were used to working— Jas, Mya, and Brent, on the other hand, started complaining halfway into it.

"Are we done yet?" Brent yelled out from his spot on the curb.

"How many more boxes do we have to carry?" Jas asked.

"I'm strong, but, dang, this is a lot of stuff," Brent added, holding his lower back. "And poor Jas can't lift any more."

"Shut up, Brent!" Jas said, elbowing Brent in the side. "I lifted just as much as you did."

"Do you think people washed these clothes before

they stuffed them into these boxes?" Mya asked. "Some of this stuff stinks."

"Okay, y'all listen . . . Ms. Grave is real cool, but she does have a mean side, so shut up before she makes us move inside with the adults," I said.

"Yeah, y'all chill out, it's not that bad," Alyssa said.

I swapped places with Jas for a while because he really did look like he was about to faint.

As the clothing drive wrapped up, I watched Kari stare down all the people carrying out bags. He'd come to replace some of the clothes he'd lost during the move. Now the only items in his size were picked over. I had to do something.

"Alyssa, I need some help," I said, motioning for her to come over away from everyone else.

"Sure," she said.

"Will you put any good clothes you have left in a box for me? Like something that would fit me."

"What are you up to?"

"I can't say, but it's kinda important."

"I got you," Alyssa said.

When the clothing drive was over, Dad arrived to pick us up. I put the box in the trunk of the SUV. Now I needed to think of a way to get the box to Kari.

"Kari, what you doing later?" I asked.

"Nothing."

"Want to come back to my house?"

"Cool."

"We could all come if that's okay with you, Mr. Walter. Wes told us you're grilling burgers," Brent said, grinning.

"Well, I have enough for three of you, but the rest of you are out of luck!" Dad teased.

We all piled into the SUV. It reminded me of the days after summer camp back when everyone lived in the same neighborhood. We would all stuff into one car, us boys smelling like rank onions—the girls complaining the whole way. We'd ride home belting out our best Drake impressions or debating who had the best layup during free play on the court.

When we got to our house, the mood changed. A grayness hung over us, like a rain cloud ready to unload. We unpacked ourselves out of the SUV and walked across the driveway. The closer we got to the front door, the grayer the air got. Alyssa's mom and Brent's and Jas's parents were all hunched together on the front porch. They were staring at a piece of paper clenched tightly in Mom's hands.

5

Mom flashed Dad a wide-eyed look—parent-speak for "We have a problem." Dad rushed us past the close-mouthed adults, into the house, and down the hall to my room.

"You guys hang out here until we call you," he instructed.

"Ummm, okay," I said under my breath as he closed my bedroom door behind him, leaving us out of whatever was going on.

I sat on the floor with my back pressed against the bed's footboard. Brent and Jas had taken over the bed, while Mya leaned against the window. Kari was propped against the closet door on the other side of the room—as far away as he could get from Mya. Alyssa sat on the floor cross-legged beside me.

The six of us hadn't been stuffed into my room at the same time in years. I just hoped the water bugs didn't decide to race each other across the floor, especially nowhere near Mya. I'd never be able to convince her we didn't have roaches—Mya has a real issue with roaches.

Once, when we were in second grade, back when Mya lived in the Oaks, Brent came up with a plan to scare her with a fake roach. When we got to school one day, he slipped the roach into her book bag, and when she pulled out her notebook, the bug fell onto the floor. She screamed. The kid next to her saw it and told the whole class Mya had roaches.

No one really believed Princess Mya had roaches, but she was still pretty mad. She knew it was me or Brent who snuck the bug into her bag, but when the teacher threatened us with a phone call to our parents, neither of us told. Brent and I always have each other's back and always end up on the same side, no matter what. We both got punished with a week of no TV, but it was worth it to see Mya scream in front of the whole class.

Back in my room, we sat quiet with the same "What do we do now?" look on our faces.

"What do you think it is?" Jas asked us, breaking the silence.

"I don't know, maybe somebody died," said Brent.

"Both of y'all shut up. Nobody's dead," Mya said.

"How do you know?" Brent asked.

"Because nobody was crying!" Mya answered, with a deep eye roll.

"Why don't we just wait until they tell us what's going on?" Alyssa chimed in.

"But it's been forever," Jas said.

"Did one of y'all steal something from the shelter?" Mya said, narrowing her eyes in Brent and Jas's direction.

"Don't start blaming us," Jas snapped.

"Well, one of y'all had to do something," Mya said.

"Mya, your white privilege is showing," Brent said.

That shut Mya right up. Jas and I tried to stuff our laughter into our palms—we failed.

Mya is *half*-white, but when she's with the crew, she tries to only show her Black side.

"What's in that box you brought back?" Brent asked, looking at me. He was just being nosy, but it still—

"Don't worry about it!" I barked.

"My bad. I'm just sayin', *I* didn't take nothing," Brent said, holding his hands in the air to prove they were empty.

"Everybody chill out," Alyssa said, with one eyebrow raised at me.

"Maybe it's nothing," Kari said.

"Right," Alyssa agreed.

"Whatever. We wouldn't be crammed into this tiny room waiting if it was nothing," Mya said, this time looking directly at Kari.

I tried to stay cool, but I could tell there was definitely something wrong. There were way too many people in this room. Suddenly I was having trouble finding air. I could taste my lunch in the back of my throat. I took slow, deep breaths. The last thing I wanted to do was puke in front of everybody.

When the door swung open, Dad led us to the living room. The air was as thick as cold grits. Mom's eyes were red. *Maybe somebody did die.* I hadn't seen Mom cry since Aunt Mabel died.

"I know you all know something is going on," Jas's mom said. "We might as well share this with you."

"Who died?" Brent blurted out.

"No one died; our neighborhood has received an offer of purchase. A development group wants to buy the land and redevelop it," Dad said, straight to the point—no sugar.

I could see one of the papers. My eyes narrowed in on SIMMONS DEVELOPMENT GROUP plastered at the top of the page.

"Wait, does that mean we won't live here anymore?" Alyssa asked. Her normally bright eyes looked sad.

"Not necessarily, this is just an offer. The board will meet and decide what to do," Mom said.

"I don't want you kids worrying about this," Alyssa's mom said. "We'll handle it. We just wanted to let you know what's going on."

A development group wants to buy the land and redevelop it. . . . I'm not stupid, that meant we'd have to move. There'd be nothing left on our block but single shoes and dirty mattresses, just like at the old apartment building.

There was no way I could leave. The Oaks is my home. I've done everything here—met my best friends, learned how to ride a bike, made my first three-pointer on the court at the park, and had so many epic hide-and-seek games—oak trees are the best for hiding. Flashes of all my favorite memories popped into my mind—a highlight reel of my life. How could I leave all that?

6

It was almost 7:00 p.m. when everyone finally left our house. Dad had gone to take Kari (and the secret box of clothes) home. I'd heard "Don't worry" eight times before the last parent walked out the door. I was tired of everyone telling me not to worry. I needed to slow my mind down and focus on something else, so I pulled out my new puzzle.

It was a birthday gift from Mr. Hank; he got me one every year now since the first one, usually something science-themed, but this was one I'd been eyeing for a long time—a 1,000-piece mash-up of my favorite Marvel superheroes.

I figured it'd take me a whole week to finish, and I'd been waiting for the right moment to get started. Now seemed like a good time. I needed to work on a challenge I could fix all on my own. Puzzles kept my mind and hands busy and somehow made me calm too.

I cracked open the seal, slid off the box top, and got to work turning all the pieces faceup. I started with the outside border of the puzzle, a strategy I read in a book once on how to be a puzzle master. The book said the picture was clearer when you focused on the outside view and then concentrated on the inner details.

I'd just finished piecing together the bottom edge when Dad got back home and called me to dinner. I wasn't really interested in talking about the offer, but that didn't matter, Mom started the conversation right as I loaded my fork with some baked beans.

"Wes, I know this is a lot for you to understand, but that's why I bring you along to so many community events. It's important for you to know what's going on around us," she said.

"Do you think we'll really have to move?" I asked.

"I won't say no, but just know there'll be a lot of people fighting to make sure Kensington Oaks is safe. The Oaks means everything to us," Mom said.

"Your mom grew up in this house," Dad said.

"I know, Dad," I said.

"Did you know Grandpa saved up for over ten years to be able to put a down payment on it?" Mom asked.

"Ten years is a long time. Almost as old as me," I said.

"Yes it is. He worked hard to own his own home," Mom said. "Back then only a few Black families lived in this neighborhood."

"For real?" I asked.

I couldn't even imagine a bunch of white people in the Oaks. There's one white family on Brent's street and one near the park, but that's it.

"Yes, when we started moving in, the white folks started moving out," Mom said.

"If this is our house and our neighborhood, how can they make us move?" I asked.

"It's not just about them making us move. It's more about us protecting our history," Dad said. "Mom's family history and the neighborhood's history are important. Even if things get uncomfortable."

"Your dad's right. We'll continue to protect our history. We have to—no one else will if we don't," Mom said.

Her steel-sharp gaze matched her words. I'd seen that look plenty of times—Mom was gearing up for a fight.

■ ■ ■

"I don't know about y'all, but I kinda like this create-your-own milk shake. I'm putting peanut butter, chocolate sauce, and M&M's in mine," Brent said the next day.

"Man, your stomach is gonna be messed up!" Jas said, frowning at Brent.

"Let me guess, you're getting a plain vanilla shake, right?" Brent asked Jas.

"Yep!" Jas said.

Alyssa, Jas, Brent, and I crowded up to a table in a corner of the new milk shake shop, Creamy Creations, with our extra-tall glasses of milky heaven. It was a new spot a few blocks from the Oaks. Next door was a build-your-own burger place, and next to that was a grind-your-own coffee café.

"So y'all think we really gonna have to move?" Jas asked.

"I'm not worried," Brent said between long sips of milk shake. "Mrs. Henderson isn't going to let that happen, right, Wes?"

I shook my head and sipped my shake.

"I don't know, there are a bunch of new buildings all around us now," Alyssa said. "My mom said it's only a matter of time."

Maybe Alyssa was right—but so was Brent. Mom wasn't going to back down.

"We can ignore the offer," Jas said. "It's not like they can break into our houses and push us out."

"No they can't, but my mom said our neighbors might sell their houses if they get paid enough," Alyssa said.

I kept trying to think of the right thing to add—but all I could think about was not wanting to move. It was like trying to come up with a reason the rec center meant so much to me, but just like then, the perfect words never came.

I stared at the icy-white walls of Creamy Creations. They were decorated with bright-colored polka dots and smiling cow faces. Every few moments the cowbell jangled as more people came inside to get their frosted milk fix. Until now, I never remembered having an ice cream shop or anything like a fancy create-your-own milk shake store near the Oaks. Mya had one of those fro-yo places, where you fill and weigh your own cups, near her house, but all we ever had was the ice cream truck that drove through our neighborhood during the summer.

We were just a few blocks from the Oaks, but everything was different over here, even the police officers. On the walk over, we passed two officers riding bikes. They looked at us real funny, but we kept our eyes straight and fast-walked by them.

A couple streets past this place was the new condo construction where Kari used to live. I guess with fancy condos going up, everything had to be new—which was nice. I mean, I'm not complaining, my milk shake was just right, but after the offer letter, I was starting to wonder what would happen if the Oaks got redeveloped. Would our street be the latest home to a bunch of stores that let you build your own pizza, bake your own doughnuts, and blend your own organic fruit smoothies?

7

Monday during social studies block, all I could think about was getting home to work on my superhero puzzle. Mr. Baker was showing images of ancient Egypt on the Smartboard, but my mind kept flashing back to the *Black Panther* corner of my puzzle and how I was one piece away from finishing it. I'd looked under every chair and in every corner, but I couldn't find the missing piece. I was glancing at the clock above the door for the third time when Mr. Baker's voice thundered my way: "Wesley, is there somewhere else you'd rather be?"

It's Wes, I wanted to say, but it was no use. At school I'm Wesley Henderson. Wes only exists in the hallways, courtyard, and café. I shook my head.

Brent's laughter from his seat on the other side of the room saved me from Mr. Baker's stare.

"Is there something funny you'd like to share with the class, Brent?" Mr. Baker asked. That's one of those questions that don't need an answer.

"No, I'm good," Brent answered anyway.

The look on Mr. Baker's face meant Brent should probably stop talking.

"Now that I have everyone's attention," Mr. Baker said, turning away from Brent and facing the class, "I'd like to tell you about your fall project. While we're learning about how world societies change over time, we'll also be learning about what's going on right here in our society and how we all fit into it. And as the year rolls on, you'll see how change never stops."

This felt like a setup for a lot of work—exactly what Mr. Baker is known for.

"With that in mind, your fall project will be about a modern issue that you feel is a changing point," Mr. Baker continued. "I want you to choose a topic about something important to you and write a report and then present your research to the class. You can choose any topic you'd like, but it has to be a modern issue or include some aspect of social justice and how it impacts today's society. Some topics students in past years have chosen include the First Amendment, marriage rights, gender equality, and protecting the ecosystem."

A report and a presentation? Great . . . I could feel the cotton mouth already.

"You'll have eight weeks to complete the entire project, but please do start thinking about your topics now," Mr. Baker said.

Grunts and *hmmm*s filled the room as Mr. Baker

handed out a piece of paper that explained the project details. Not one sixth grader was happy about the idea of a fall project—well, maybe Alyssa.

"Does the topic have to directly impact us?" she asked, right on cue.

"That's a great question," Mr. Baker said. Alyssa always asks good questions. "It doesn't have to directly impact you, but I hope during your research you will find a common link to your life. The completed assignment should include a two-page report and a ten-minute presentation on what you learned during your research."

Not only did I have to pick a topic interesting enough to write two pages on, I had to give a ten-minute presentation in front of the whole class. Sixth grade was turning out to be harder than I expected. One good thing was we'd have two whole months to work on it, so I pushed it out of my mind and waited for the ending bell to ring.

■ ■ ■

During lunch the next day, Jas convinced me to meet him in the band room to listen to his drum solo. Jas plays the snare drum and is section leader in the Grove's marching band, which is unusual for a sixth grader, but he's that good. At the end of his audition over the summer, Mr. Towns, the band director, begged Jas to join the band—well, that's what his mom said.

The stuffy band room was not exactly where I wanted to spend my lunch, but it was better than listening to Alyssa talk about her women's rights idea (yep, she'd already picked a topic) and listening to Brent go through a list of ideas that had nothing to do with social justice. Plus, this solo was a big deal for Jas; he had arranged the whole thing by himself. He's like a musical scholar. He studies drumbeats the way I study puzzles.

He's figured out his life plan: he wants to be a producer—his music, with someone else performing over the beat. It's the perfect combo, since he can't sing or rap but as a producer he can be fully into the music culture without being in the spotlight.

Jas and I had the band room all to ourselves, and he got busy on the drums as soon as I sat down.

"So what you think?" he asked when he was done.

"It was good," I answered.

"Good? I need more than that," he said.

"More?" I wasn't sure what he wanted me to say; all his sets were good to me.

"Close your eyes and listen," he said. "Tell me how it makes you feel."

He started again. This time I closed my eyes and concentrated on the music.

Sticks *tip-tap*ped against the drums.

Bass vibrated through the floor and up the walls.

Cymbals rang out short, sharp tones.

Sound echoed from every corner of the room, wrapping itself around me.

"Yeah, it's better than good," I said when the set crashed to an end. "It's powerful. Kinda like how it feels after I beat you in NBA 2K."

Jas just looked back at me with a satisfied smile. He was going to rock the solo.

8

After dinner that night, the whole neighborhood loaded into the community center for a board meeting about the Simmons offer. The community center is an old building at the back of the Oaks, five blocks over from our house. It's just a big, open room with wood-paneled walls that make it seem darker than it really is. And there's always a dusty smell in the air.

The center used to be a hangout spot for neighborhood kids to use after school or on the weekends, to play ball or study. That was before some of the older kids got caught smoking inside the building. After that, no one was allowed inside without a community board member.

I hadn't seen this many people pile into the center ever. Everyone was mad about the offer letter, and this meeting was for them to talk things out. Plastic chairs were arranged in rows across the length of the room. Most everybody decided to stand, because the plastic chairs would stick to your butt in this crazy heat.

Loud talking started before the meeting even got

going. It turned out everyone had an opinion about what to do, and all those opinions were different.

"I call this meeting to order at 6:05 p.m.," Mom said. "Please take a seat and let's go over the agenda. First the board will provide all the information we have so far. Then we've invited Carla Glass from Simmons Development Group to answer any questions we have on their offer. Lastly, we'll talk about next steps. I ask that we all respect each other."

Mom couldn't even finish reading the letter everyone had received before people started talking again, but they did at least take a seat.

I searched the room for my friends—nope, no one, not even Alyssa. I should've known none of them would be caught dead at a community board meeting.

"Here's what we know so far," Mom said. "The current terms of this offer are good for sixty days. I recommend we have a unified front. Let's come up with a standard response."

"What will the response say?" someone from the crowd yelled out.

"That's what we are here to talk about," Mom explained, but no one was listening.

"The offer for my house is more than market value. If we reject it, we could get less money later," someone called out.

"Right!" someone else agreed. "And they may not make another offer."

So much for a standard response. Everyone started talking over each other again. Mr. Hank tried to calm the crowd: "Listen, if everybody settles down, we'll all get to speak."

"Yeah," I said under my breath, agreeing with Mr. Hank.

"Look, if I can get paid more than my house is worth, I want the money!" another neighbor yelled. "What are you doing here, anyway?" she asked, looking directly at me.

I swallowed my smart-aleck response and slunk away to the other side of the room.

Mom tossed a worried look in my direction. She hadn't heard what that lady said, but she had to see the steam puffing from my ears.

"It's about more than the money. What about our neighborhood's legacy and heritage?" That was Jas's mom, Mrs. Silva.

Tap, tap, tap. Mom banged a small mallet on the table. "There seem to be a lot of questions, so let's welcome Carla Glass."

Dad escorted Ms. Glass into the room. Everyone's eyes turned toward her.

Ms. Glass was a small, pale-skinned woman with

spiked brown hair. I stared at her pointy heels and wondered how she'd made it across the gravel driveway without tipping over.

She *click-clack*ed across the floor and stood beside Mom. "Thank you for allowing me to be a part of these important discussions," she said. "I realize this is a very hard decision, and I'd like to answer any questions you have."

Several people jumped to their feet.

"If we accept the offer, how much prior notice will we get before our move-out date?" Brent's dad called out.

"That's something we'll negotiate with each homeowner separately," Ms. Glass explained. "Which could be a long process, but ideally, Simmons Development Group would take possession of the land sometime before the end of the year."

My heart dropped. *The end of the year? That's only a couple months away.*

"What if we all reject your offer?" Mr. Hank asked.

"Well, we've prepared a very convincing offer," she said. "In fact, we're in the last phase of negotiations with the neighboring community, Carolina Farms."

"Oh no," I said to myself.

"What are you planning to build on our land?" Mr. Hank asked.

"We'd like to build two new multifamily dwellings and a small retail center. I will be more than happy to share the renderings with you."

"Multifamily dwellings? That's fancy talk for a condo building for rich people!" Mr. Silva yelled from the back of the room.

Most people must have been thinking the same thing, because more and more neighbors started shouting out of turn or fussing at each other.

"You can leave now! We aren't selling!"

"Wait, you can't speak for all of us. . . ."

"What about me? I'm a renter."

This meeting was getting out of hand. Mom decided to let Ms. Glass go before things got ugly. After another hour of yelling, the group came up with a list of responses to vote on at the next meeting.

It was 8:30 p.m. when I left the community center. This wasn't going to be an easy fight.

9

The next day, after school, I decided to look into all the new buildings going up around Kensington Oaks. Ms. Glass from Simmons had said they were working with Carolina Farms, but I wondered if they were looking at other neighborhoods around ours too.

I asked Alyssa to meet me at the library on the block over from the Oaks. She was the smartest out of our crew, and I needed her to help me figure this stuff out—plus, I wasn't even sure Jas and Brent thought the offer was something we should be worried about.

I cut through the path behind Mr. Hank's house to get there. The path used to be an official pass-through that joined the Oaks with the next street, which housed the library and corner store. But it's overgrown, and since the corner store closed a couple years ago, people barely use it anymore.

The branches swept my arms and face as I walked along the path. It's the only cool spot in the Oaks on a hot day. The sun barely peeked through the mini-forest of trees—in the right area, a slight breeze might even blow by. In this very spot, I had almost gotten my first kiss. *Almost* being the most important word.

It was the last day of fifth grade, and Brent had dared me to kiss Ava Sánchez. I didn't really like Ava like that, but the rumor was she liked me. Since the dare was loud enough for the whole class to hear, I *had* to go through with it. After class, Ava and I went onto the path. We stood under the trees, staring at each other with wide eyes. I figured I should make the first move, so I inched closer, leaned in, and closed my eyes. A wet smooch landed on the tip of my nose. I opened my eyes just in time to find Ava *and* Brent running off the path, laughing. I still don't know if it was Brent or Ava who kissed my nose.

Shaking the memory away, I got to the library first and dragged two lopsided chairs over to the computer desk at the back of the room. We had the place to ourselves, except for an occasional teacher-looking lady checking out books.

"What are we doing here?" Alyssa asked when she sat down.

"Not sure exactly. Looking for anything we can find about Simmons Development Group. At the board meeting last night, the lady from Simmons said they had already bought some other land around the city."

Being in the library made me remember all the story circles Mom used to lead here. She was head librarian when I went to Oak Gardens Elementary, before she became leader of the community board. She insisted I meet her at the library after school every day. I would rather have hung out with my friends in the neighborhood, but nope, she wasn't having it. Instead, I'd take the short, lonely walk over to the library by myself.

It was usually just me and Mom. Aside from a special meeting or program, the place didn't get much use. When I got too bored I'd hide between the long rows of books and sneak a nap, which lasted no longer than fifteen minutes before Mom called me to help sort and stock the shelves. The only good thing that came from my time in library jail was I'd become a master librarian. I could restock a stack of books in minutes and research any topic.

Alyssa logged on, started a Google search, and typed in *Simmons Development Group*. She got *37,300,000 results.* She clicked on the first link—some place in Tennessee called Simmons Property Group—not the same people.

Then, after clicking on the third article, Alyssa said, "Wes, look—Simmons Development Group is the same developer for that new condo building downtown."

A knot started to grow in my stomach. *That's the same building we've been marching to stop. The same building where Kari used to live.* The knot got bigger. Between our neighbors fighting and Ms. Glass saying they wanted to take possession this year, I wondered if we really had a chance.

Alyssa and I spent the next two hours reading every article we could find on Simmons Development Group. Simmons *had* been busy clearing out land right near us.

I was just about to log off when I noticed something in an article I'd just finished reading.

"What's Mr. Baker's first name?" I asked, turning to Alyssa.

"Why? His teacher badge says Brian . . . no . . . Byron. Byron Baker."

"Read this, an article in the *Observer*, 'Is Gentrification the New Segregation?' It says when neighborhoods are renovated to appeal to richer residents, it's called gentrification." I'd heard that word before, at some of the marches, but seeing it spelled out made it feel way more real.

"It's the cause of many poor families being forced to move," I said, continuing to read the article. "This was written by a middle school teacher named Byron Baker."

"That has to be him," Alyssa said.

"That's what happened to Kari. The same thing will happen to us if we don't fix this."

I wasn't sure what we were up against, but I had a good idea where to start.

■ ■ ■

The next morning during homeroom, I couldn't wait to get Mr. Baker alone. After announcements and attendance, I cornered him to ask about his article on gentrification. He told me to come back after school. I couldn't tell if he was mad or grumpy or just being Mr. Baker, but he said, "We should talk about this later."

I could barely stay focused during math—I mean, how is the absolute value of -5, 5? I spent my lunch period in the school's library. It was the perfect place to be alone. Maybe it was Kari, or maybe it was all those marches Mom had forced me to go to, but a fire was rising in my belly. The offer letter from Simmons Development Group was the kindling; the information in Mr. Baker's article was the firewood. I needed to find a way to put this fire out.

I was reading over Mr. Baker's article again when Brent strolled into the library.

"You didn't come to lunch," he said.

"I know. I'm reading up on this stuff about the development group," I said.

"My dad said we could make some real money by

selling our houses." Brent's words hit me hard, like a brick.

"What? Selling our houses?"

"I'm just telling you what he told me." Brent tossed his arms in the air.

"Brent, that's crazy. We can't give up our neighborhood. They'll just build another condo building. Where will that leave us?"

"Dang, Wes, chill. I'm just staying it would be nice to have some extra money."

I knew Brent hadn't seemed all that upset about the offer, but I couldn't believe his parents would even think about selling their house, and Brent seemed like he was down with it. He has one of the best yards in the Oaks. It has the perfect number of trees. And his first-ever pet frog, Jumper, is buried under the big tree in his backyard—we'd had a funeral for him and everything. How could Brent be okay with moving away?

"I gotta go," I said, storming past Brent.

I left the library with a pukey feeling low in my gut.

After school, I went to Mr. Baker's classroom. My brain was overloaded with so many things. I needed answers.

I found Mr. Baker sitting behind his desk, looking toward the door—almost like he was waiting for me. I'd never asked a teacher for help on something not about school stuff, but I took a deep breath and started talking—spitting out all at once that I'd read his article on gentrification and we needed to save the Oaks.

"Whoa. Wesley, let's back up," said Mr. Baker. "Why don't you start from the beginning?"

I started again. "I read your article, and the stuff you wrote about is happening in my neighborhood, Kensington Oaks. A development group made an offer to buy our houses, but we don't want to move—I for sure don't want to move."

"Okay, go on."

"You said gentrification is the new segregation. We need to stop it."

Mr. Baker motioned for me to sit down. Then he leaned toward me.

"I didn't say gentrification was the new segregation; I posed the question. I wrote that article to start a conversation about ways to combat unfair displacement."

"It is unfair! That's why we have to stop it."

My voice was starting to rise.

"There's no way to stop gentrification, Wesley."

"So do we give up?" I asked, my voice completely raised.

"Not at all. You need to collect the facts first, and then you need a plan. Have you talked to your parents about this?"

"Kinda, not really," I said. "I went to the community board meeting, but that was just a bunch of yelling."

"Talk to them. And there are some city organizations you can team up with," Mr. Baker said. "Wesley, I am proud of you for standing up for your community." Mr. Baker's usually booming voice was a bit softer.

"Thanks, Mr. Baker," I said, turning to walk away.

For some reason, that made me feel better. I've never felt close to any of my teachers, and not that they don't like me, but they don't pay me any attention either way. I'm not super smart like Alyssa or funny like Brent. Yeah, I was Best Dressed, but teachers don't care about that kind of thing.

Mr. Baker seemed different. He never picked favorites, and you couldn't tell who he liked or didn't like. For all I knew, he didn't like anybody—but he'd just said he was proud of me. Maybe that meant something, maybe not.

10

I called a meeting the next day after school—I wanted to put together my own team before I talked to Mom about joining the fight. I met Brent, Jas, Alyssa, Mya, and Kari in Mr. Baker's classroom.

"Wes, what's this about?" Mya asked.

"And why is he here?" Brent whispered in my direction, tipping his head toward Mr. Baker.

"This is important, guys," I said, ignoring Brent and Mya. "Y'all want to stay in the Oaks, right?"

"What does this have to do with the Oaks?" Jas asked.

"Didn't y'all hear about the board meeting?" I asked. "Everyone was fighting and yelling. I don't think the board is going to be able to fix all this."

That got their attention.

"Was it really that bad?" Jas asked.

"Yeah, it was pretty bad," I said. "We should be doing something to help."

Mr. Baker came over from behind his desk to join us. I told them he knew some community organizations that could help.

"That's right; I've worked with a group called Save

Our City. They'd be able to get you started on the right track," said Mr. Baker.

"Are y'all in?" I asked.

"Count me out. This sounds like too much trouble. Besides, I don't live in Kensington Oaks anymore," said Mya.

"Are you sure you want to fight these people?" Jas said. "I'm in, but what if we lose?"

"We should at least try. We'll definitely lose if we don't try," Alyssa added. "I'm in."

"Wes, you know I got your back," Kari said.

So it was me, Alyssa, Jas, and Kari.

"My dad said we could use the money to buy a bigger house. I can't go against my dad," Brent said.

"So you're out?" I asked. I couldn't believe Brent was leaving me hanging. That stung—Brent's always been on my side.

"Yeah, I'm out," Brent said.

■ ■ ■

Mr. Baker contacted his friend at Save Our City to help with saving the Oaks. We'd have to wait a whole week to meet her, but in the meantime, we turned Mr. Baker's classroom into our headquarters—our safe place. Every day after school, we met to share any new information we found. Mr. Baker was cool about it and didn't bother us too much. He just sat in the back of the room grading papers.

I'd read Mr. Baker's article so many times I'd memorized most of the sections word for word. But I still wasn't sure how gentrification had anything to do with segregation.

Jas must have been confused too, 'cause while we were coming up with a list of questions to ask Mr. Baker's friend, he asked, "Why don't they just redevelop their own neighborhoods?"

He had a point. "Mr. Baker, why do they want to come to our neighborhood?" I asked.

"All right, guys and lady, time for a little history lesson," Mr. Baker said. "Back in the 1960s, after the desegregation of schools, lots of white families started leaving cities and moving to the suburbs."

"To get away from Black people?" I asked.

"You could say that," Mr. Baker said. "That left the inner cities full of lower-income people, mostly Black and brown people. In the past several years, that dynamic has started changing again."

"That's messed up," I said.

"Where'd you grow up, Mr. Baker?" Alyssa asked.

"I grew up in a neighborhood like Kensington Oaks, about ten miles from here."

"But you're not Black . . . or brown," Jas said, looking confused.

Mr. Baker smiled. "Well, Jasper, that's true, but growing up in a community similar to yours taught me to be an ally and a friend and fight beside my neighbors."

"That's why you married a Black lady?" Kari asked. Jas and I looked wide-eyed at Kari and tried to hide our laughs. We didn't really know if Mr. Baker was married, and we definitely didn't know if he was married to a Black lady, but someone had made up the story and now everyone repeated it.

"Okay, enough about me. I need to get back to grading, and you have some reading to do. I found an article that would be good for you to check out."

"Oooh, man," Kari groaned as Mr. Baker passed around the article.

Jas and I slapped Kari on the back of the head at exactly the same time.

"This is your fault," I whispered loudly.

"And why would you bring up his wife?" Jas asked. "It's probably not even true."

Kari didn't bother to turn around. He put the article on the desk in front of him and started reading.

■ ■ ■

The next week, Mr. Baker introduced us to his friend. "Everyone, this is Ms. Monica Greene," he said, walking a lady into his classroom.

Ms. Monica wore a silky brown pantsuit and a glittery gold bow tie—I'd never seen a lady wear a bow tie, but I kinda liked it. She had wavy burgundy hair that fell past her shoulders, and bright pink lipstick popped against her light brown skin.

"Nice to meet y'all," Ms. Monica said in a sugary voice.

"Can you help us save our neighborhood?" I blurted out.

"You must be Wesley," she said, reaching out a hand to me. "I hope I can help. Tell me a little about what's going on."

I filled her in about what was happening in the Oaks, about the offer, and about how some neighbors wanted to sell and some didn't.

"That's tricky," Ms. Monica said.

"If we can convince everyone not to sell, maybe Simmons will go away," Alyssa said.

Ms. Monica sighed. "I wish that were the case, but that's not likely," she said. "Kensington Oaks is located in a prime area for revitalization—it's just blocks from the city center. That's the reason Simmons made an offer."

"Ms. Monica, I read an article that said gentrification can be good. Is that true?" Alyssa asked.

"The benefits are mainly financial. Typically, a developer—like Simmons—purchases land in urban areas where lower-income people live. Some of these areas are run-down, so the property values are cheap. That makes it easy for the developer to buy low, redevelop, and sell high."

"But how does that help us?" I asked.

"Well, when construction is done, there will be new homes, restaurants, and shops," Ms. Monica explained. "That will bring more revenue and more jobs to the area."

"That does sound good, except for the part about us being kicked out of our homes," Alyssa said. "Any changes should help the people who already live here."

"Right. And the new properties will be more expensive. That means most of the families who have to leave wouldn't be able to afford to go back there to live," Ms. Monica said.

How is that fair! I wanted to scream.

"Can we fix up our own neighborhood ourselves and stay here?" I asked.

"That's a great question, Wesley. That's one of the missions of Save Our City. But I have to be honest, that's a very expensive and sometimes difficult solution."

"My mom says the best solutions are always the hardest," Alyssa said.

"I suggest you get a tally of how many people are

willing to sell. That will help us decide what to do next," Ms. Monica said.

"Okay, guys, let's thank Ms. Monica for her time," Mr. Baker said. "Monica, we'll be in touch with any new information." He led her into the hallway.

"So what do we do now?" Jas asked.

"I'll talk to my mom and see if the board has done a poll of who wants to stay and who wants to sell," I said.

"We'll save the Oaks, Wes—we got this," Alyssa said.

"Yeah, we got this," said Kari.

■ ■ ■

That night in bed, a twenty-pound weight pressed on my chest. Twenty pounds of guilt. I tossed back and forth, trying to get it to ease. It wouldn't go away. *I'm a horrible friend*—I'd turned my back on Kari when his family had to move, and here he was, still on my team. I'd thought the condo building downtown wasn't that bad. If only someone had stopped Simmons before now, maybe they wouldn't have come for the Oaks.

11

On our way to school Monday morning, Alyssa, Brent, Jas, and I took our usual walk down my block, through the neighborhood park, toward the Grove. Just as we reached the park, we spotted Ms. Elise, from the board, tacking up signs that read WE AREN'T LEAVING.

This was her second batch of signs—the first batch had been crossed out with red spray paint and some ripped down completely. I didn't believe him at first, but Dad said it had to be someone from the Oaks who messed up the signs.

The four of us sped by Ms. Elise as she fussed to herself about "people having no respect."

When we were far enough past her, Brent said, "Dang, I've never seen her mad before."

He was right. Ms. Elise usually had a smile for every-one, but I'd heard Mom talking about all the neighbors who were interested in accepting the Simmons offer and that she'd even had to cut the last board meeting short because everyone was screaming again.

• • •

On my way to first block, I was thinking about how we'd never save the Oaks with everyone fighting.

First block was math. I hate math.

I hated math even more with Ms. Hardy teaching it. She only liked the smart kids—and I'm not smart, at least not in math.

"What in the world is *Math Jeopardy!*?" I whispered to Alyssa when I got to my seat. Ms. Hardy had colored letters pinned to the whiteboard that spelled out *Math Jeopardy!*

"I don't know," Alyssa whispered back from her seat in front of me. "Sounds kinda fun, though." Of course Alyssa thought a math game would be fun.

It turned out *Math Jeopardy!* was *Jeopardy!* but with math questions or equations to solve.

Ms. Hardy read questions from a podium in the front of the room, Alex Trebek–style. You could holler out your answer, or if you needed to work out an equation, you could use the board. The first person with the correct answer won points. Alyssa and I went against each other in the first round.

Ms. Hardy read out, "If Sky's lunch cost sixty dollars and fifty cents and she gave a twenty percent tip, how much did she spend?"

My first thought was *What did Sky eat that cost sixty dollars and fifty cents?* Before I could even write out the equation on the board, Alyssa called out, "Seventy-two dollars and sixty cents!"

Of course she was right—she'd one-upped me in NBA 2K and now in math equations.

I missed my next question too.

Math block sped by with most of the class acting like they were actually having fun. Right before the bell rang, I was called up for my last question.

"Taye had nine dollars and fifty cents. He spent two seventy-five on candy and gave his two friends a dollar seventy-five each," Ms. Hardy read. "How much money was left?"

I had this one.

"Three dollars and twenty-five cents!" I screamed out before Jamie, the guy going against me.

"Good job!" Ms. Hardy said.

Alyssa gave me a little cheer from her seat, and for a second I forgot how much I hated math. I came back to my senses by lunchtime and figured it out—*Math Jeopardy!* was all a trick to make us think math wasn't so bad. I guess a little fun makes even horrible things seem better.

■ ■ ■

I had an idea for the first time since the offer and felt excited about something we could do. We met after school in Mr. Baker's room. Even Ms. Monica came.

"Maybe we could do something fun to get everyone to stop fighting," I said, thinking back to *Math Jeopardy!* After seeing Ms. Elise get all mad about her signs, we definitely needed a way to chill everyone out.

Everybody got into it right away and started calling out ideas.

"What about a basketball tournament?" Kari asked.

"Nah, too many old people," I said.

"We could have a talent show . . . ," Alyssa said.

"Nah, not enough talent," I said, shaking my head.

"Well, you come up with an idea," Alyssa said, turning toward me.

"It needs to be fun . . . like a party," I said. "What about a block party? Like we had last summer after the hurricane. Remember Brent hit the winning ball that dunked Mr. York into the dunking booth?"

We all laughed. Mr. York, my neighbor, was sure none of us had good enough aim to sink him, and then came Brent. Maybe a party would chill out the weirdness with me and Brent too.

"Yeah! That was fun," Jas said. "We should definitely have another block party!"

"We'll need music," Kari said. "And we can have a slideshow of pictures from the good days in the Oaks."

"Before all the fighting," Alyssa added.

"I can handle the music," Jas said.

"Me and Kari can work on the slideshow," I said.

"I'll make the signs and decorations," Alyssa chimed in.

"What about food?" Kari asked.

"Save Our City will sponsor the food and drinks and take care of the permit," said Ms. Monica.

I could see the pieces sliding into place. The only way to beat Simmons Development Group was as one complete team. I couldn't wait to get home and tell Mom and Dad about the block party. We'd need them to help pull it off.

■ ■ ■

Mom and Dad were sprawled out on the couch watching the news.

"I have something I need to talk to you about," I said.

"Sure, Wes. What is it?" Dad asked, sitting up straight.

"Jas, Alyssa, Kari, and I have been working on a plan to save the Oaks."

"Son, we told you not to worry about that," Dad said.

There was no way I couldn't be worried—the Oaks is my home too.

"I know, but Mr. Baker, my social studies teacher,

and Ms. Monica know a bunch of people who can help us."

"Who's Ms. Monica?" Mom asked.

"She's from Save Our City."

"I've heard of that organization," Mom said. "They do great work. They always sponsor a booth at the shelter's annual food drive."

"She's on our team. Ms. Monica says since only some of our neighbors are willing to accept the offer, we have a chance of changing their minds."

"I've talked to them, honey. A lot of them don't want their minds changed," Mom said.

"Well, we have to try, and . . . I was thinking we could have a block party," I said.

"A block party?" Dad asked.

"Yeah, to get everyone to stop fighting," I said. I could tell Dad wasn't sure about the block party idea, but I did see a little sparkle in Mom's eye. "We think it'll get everyone talking again and remind them why we all like living in the Oaks."

"That is actually a great idea, Wes," Mom said.

"Really?" I asked.

"Yes, really." Mom smiled and gave me a hug. "Your dad and I will do anything we can to help."

Now that Mom and Dad were in, we had two weeks to plan the dopest block party Kensington Oaks had ever seen.

■ ■ ■

It was Taco Tuesday—my absolute favorite day in the café. After Brent, Jas, and I stacked our tortillas with loads of beef and cheese, we headed to our normal table. Alyssa and Mya were waiting on us, each with an identical version of the plainest lunch ever. A turkey sandwich, string cheese tube, baked potato chips, and a banana—our tacos beat their lunch by a mile.

We spent our whole lunch talking about the block party. I'd already started collecting pictures for the slideshow, and Alyssa was trying to decide what color decorations we should use. Now we just needed some fun stuff for us kids.

"Let's have a bounce house," Jas said.

"Bounce houses are for babies," Brent said. "You should bring back the dunking booth."

"It's only fun if the adults get in, and after you sent Mr. York into that dirty water last time, there is no way he'll do it again," Alyssa said.

"Okay, what about a water balloon fight?" Brent asked. He was acting more excited than any of us, considering he wasn't helping us with the plan to stop Simmons.

"So what's the point of the block party anyway?" Mya asked. She'd been sitting there trying to ignore us the whole time, but I guess she'd had enough of our loud talking.

"We're trying to get everyone to stop fighting," Alyssa said.

"Who's fighting?" Mya asked.

"Everybody," Jas said. "Did you hear that Brent's dad and Mr. Hank got in each other's face at the last meeting?"

"That's not true," Brent said, glaring at Jas.

"Well, that's what my mom told my dad," Jas said. "And Ms. Elise was about to flip the other day."

That only made Mya more irritated, and now Brent was frowning too.

"So the party is to get everyone thinking about the good times we've had in the Oaks," I said, trying to cool the air, but I could tell Mya didn't care about how great the Oaks was.

"Maybe it's a good thing people are thinking about moving," she said. "There *are* other places to live, you know?"

I didn't answer.

"Some of us don't have a choice about moving," Brent said.

"Well, we're planning a party for the people who do have a choice . . . ," I said.

"What does that mean?" Brent asked, sticking his chest out in my direction.

"It means the party will be awesome!" Alyssa said before I could answer.

I swallowed my answer to Brent—maybe he didn't have a choice, but some of us did, and we were choosing to save the Oaks.

. . .

The next day after school, the team met in Mr. Baker's classroom to make a flyer for the block party. It was time to get the word out. Our flyer had to be good enough to convince everybody to come to the party even though some of them were mad.

I'd started on my own draft; I just needed to get the team's okay before we printed it.

IT'S A PAAAAAARTY!
THE DOPEST PARTY THE OAKS HAS EVER SEEN
EVEN BETTER THAN LAST YEAR!
DON'T MISS IT, NEXT SATURDAY AT 4:00
IF YOU HAVE AN ATTITUDE . . . STAY HOME!

"We can't use that! It's mean. . . . We're trying to get the community together, remember?" Alyssa said.

"What? This is a great flyer," I said, defending my hard work.

"Jas, Kari, please tell him," Alyssa said.

"Well . . . I don't love it . . . the part about the at-titude *is* kinda mean," Jas said.

"What's mean about it? You know people have attitudes," I said. "Kari, what do you think?"

"I'm with Alyssa. We want to bring everyone to-gether, right?" Kari asked.

"The party was my idea, so I should be able to pick what goes on the flyer," I snapped back.

"Talk about attitude . . . ," Alyssa said, smirking at me.

"Time out, guys," Mr. Baker said. "This is a team effort, and you need to work on the flyer together." He looked at me.

"Right!" Alyssa said.

"Why don't we all make a flyer and we'll vote on the best one," Jas suggested.

"That's a good idea, Jasper," Mr. Baker said.

Everyone picked a corner of the classroom and got to work on the flyers. Mine was already good, so I didn't change it, but Alyssa, Jas, and Kari came up with their own ideas.

This was Alyssa's:

Come Join Us!
WHAT: A block party in Kensington Oaks
WHEN: Next Saturday at 4:00 PM
WHY: To bring the neighborhood together
Hope to see you there!

BOOOORING!!!

This was Jas's:

PARTY TIME!
COME TO OUR PARTY!
WE'LL HAVE MUSIC AND DANCING!
FEATURING DJ JAS!
NEXT SATURDAY AT 4:00

Not bad, but not as good as mine.

This was Kari's:

WE'RE HAVING A BLOCK PARTY
TO GET THE OAKS BACK TOGETHER
NEXT SATURDAY AT 4:00 IN THE PARK
WE'LL HAVE FOOD AND FUN!

It was okay, but something was missing.

"Why don't you use something from all of your flyers?" Mr. Baker suggested. "And have you thought of a theme? It would be nice to have a theme for the party."

Good thing Mr. Baker was there, because I hadn't thought about a theme, and without him we would've never agreed on a flyer. Here is what we decided on:

IT'S A PARTY TO BRING THE NEIGHBORHOOD TOGETHER!
JOIN US FOR THE DOPEST BLOCK PARTY TO EVER HIT THE OAKS!
NEXT SATURDAY IN THE PARK AT 4:00 PM
WE'LL HAVE MUSIC, DANCING, AND, YES, THERE WILL BE FOOD!
COME READY TO HAVE FUN!

It was just right! We made copies at the library and spent the rest of the afternoon tacking flyers to every tree in the Oaks—well, maybe not every tree, but a lot of trees.

12

The next afternoon on the walk home from school, Brent brought up the social justice project. I'd been too busy planning the block party to think about it, and we still had six weeks until it was due. Brent had switched his topic from climate change to gun control, then finally settled on protecting the First Amendment. Alyssa was halfway done with her paper already. I still didn't have a topic.

"For my presentation, I'm thinking about recording a video," Alyssa said.

"That sounds like way too much work for a little project," Brent said.

"It's not a little project," Alyssa said. "And Mr. Baker expects our best."

"When did he tell you that?" Brent asked. "Oh, let me guess—when y'all were hanging out in his room after school?" His words were mean, even for Brent.

"He's been helping us with the block party," I said. "You didn't want to help, remember?"

"So he's your best friend, right?" Brent said, looking at me.

"My best friend? You trying to be funny?" I said.

"Can both of you chill?" Alyssa asked, looking back and forth between me and Brent.

"He's the one that got all mad," Brent said.

I wasn't mad!

I didn't even bother to correct him, though. Plus, I didn't really know what to say—maybe I *was* mad. I'd only gotten mad at Brent one other time, back in third grade when he didn't pick me first to be on his basketball team during gym.

Something was going on with him. Or me. Or both of us. Or maybe we really weren't on the same side anymore.

■ ■ ■

A couple of days later, I strolled over to the community park to meet Brent and Jas—it's usually my favorite part of every weekend, hanging with the guys at the park. There isn't much to do there except shoot hoops on the basketball court, if you can even call it a court. With its stained, cracked pavement and rusted rims, it has seen better days.

The weekends meant high school kids would be at the park, hanging around looking for somebody to bother. Nothing me and my crew couldn't handle, but still, it would be nice to chill without fighting for a spot or to keep your ball.

I got there first. Good, keeping your spot was easier than trying to get someone to share theirs or waiting for the older guys to get bored enough to leave. I bounced my worn ball down the brick path and around the old fountain, between my legs, in and out, back and forth, while I waited on Jas and Brent. My new ball had better grip, but bringing a new ball on the weekend was nothing less than stupid.

"Wassup?" I called out as Jas ran across the court.

"Hey!" Jas said, slapping my hand.

"You seen Brent?"

"Nah."

"HORSE until he shows up?"

"Yeah, let's get it."

I chest-passed the ball to Jas.

Swish! His first basket was good. A simple layup.

Swish! I followed up with a layup of my own.

We traded a couple more easy shots before I upped the competition with a long-range three.

Splash! Nothing but net.

Clank. Jas's shot bounced off the backboard and just missed the rim. The ball rolled across the court, stopping right in front of a pair of the largest LeBron 10s I had seen up close—they belonged to Drip.

Drip is at least six three. He towers over all the kids in the neighborhood.

Apparently, after God blessed him with height, he

forgot to bless him with brains. Drip is supposed to be in the eleventh grade, but he started this school year as a ninth grader. That was before he got suspended for stealing a teacher's cell phone. At some point, they'll kick him out forever.

"Brick!" Drip laughed and pointed at Jas. "Dang, li'l man, you gotta come better than that. I'll tell you what . . . I'll give you another chance to make that shot and you can keep your ball. You miss, and I get the ball and your spot on the court."

"Let me take the shot for him," I pleaded.

"Nope, he has to do it," Drip said, looking at Jas.

I looked around to see if Brent was close by; at least he could talk Drip down. Brent has a way of keeping the older guys calm, maybe because he's almost as tall as them. I couldn't remember a time I'd gotten my ball taken when Brent was around. I still couldn't believe he'd left us hanging.

Drip picked the ball up and threw it across the court. It came flying at Jas, just missing his face. Jas barely caught the ball. His hands were shaky and sweating— no way he was going to make that shot.

He rubbed his wet hands, one after the other, on the front of his shorts and took a deep breath. He bounced the ball against the pavement, bent his knees, jumped, and hurled the ball toward the basket.

Clank.

I watched as my ball rolled off the pavement and into the grass. I knew that was the last time I would see it.

"Guess I got a new ball!" Drip laughed.

Jas and I turned to walk away while Drip practiced layups with my ball in my spot. Brent had completely ghosted.

13

Monday afternoon I found myself sitting on my front step, waiting for Kari. We were supposed to be working on the slideshow for the block party, but I hadn't seen him at school earlier. *Maybe something happened at the hotel.* I wasn't even sure I wanted to know.

Then it was like someone had poured my thoughts right out, because Kari strolled up the street, looking as chill as ever.

"Kari? Where've you been?"

"Danica was sick, so I had to stay home with her today 'cause my mom had to work."

"Oh, okay." I knew better than to ask any more questions. Kari was sensitive about his little sister, Danica.

"Let's get started on the slideshow," Kari said.

We went inside and got busy working on the show.

We uploaded and sorted pictures we'd gotten from our moms. There was even a picture of me and Kari when we were babies. Well, I was a baby and Kari was a little kid. He was trying to hold me on his lap. Some-times I forgot how far back me and Kari went.

"Do you think Mya and Brent will come to the block party?" Kari asked, pulling my mind away from the picture.

"Brent will definitely be there. He'd never miss a party. Mya? Probably not. She doesn't claim the Oaks anymore." I shrugged but then decided to just go ahead and say what I'd been thinking. "Kari, thanks for having my back. You don't even live here anymore, but you're still helping."

"You're my little bro. You know everything about me and my family and never once treated me different. I know people call me weird, but you hang with me anyway. I miss being in the Oaks—I feel a little left out not living here anymore."

A twinge of guilt stabbed at my side as I thought back to the times I hadn't invited Kari over when Mya was around. The truth is, I had been treating Kari dif-ferent lately. I don't even know exactly when I'd quit having his back, but that had to stop.

"How's it living in that hotel?" I asked.

"Noisy. There're always different people hanging around. Mom is scared for Danica to play outside. She's thinking about moving us to live with my aunt."

"What? Man, that's like two hours away."

"I know, but we don't have anywhere else to go.

Plus, my little cousins are the same age as Danica, so she'll have someone to play with."

"What about you?"

"It's not about me." Kari had a faraway look in his eyes. "Anyway, let's get back to this slideshow."

14

The rest of the week zoomed by and it was Saturday just like that. The block party was starting in just a couple hours. The crew and I rushed to get the final decorations up. Alyssa had picked the theme, "Take Back the Block." It was perfect—that was exactly what we were doing, taking back our block, and we'd need the whole neighborhood for that.

We hung a huge sign flanked by gold and purple balloons at the entrance of the neighborhood. We tacked gold arrows to tree trunks to point everyone in the direction of the park. Balloons and streamers, tied in trees, waved above us. Mr. Hank helped me and Jas set up speakers and a projection screen for the slideshow. The park would be party central.

Mr. Baker, Ms. Monica, and her friends from Save Our City arrived with the food. We'd picked a menu of southern barbecue favorites: pulled pork, beef brisket, baked beans, buttered corn on the cob, corn bread muffins, and peach cobbler for dessert. Jas had the awesome idea of setting up the food in a couple different areas so everyone would have to walk around and talk to each other.

Mom could hardly keep her hands still. "Wes, I am so proud," she said, reaching to hug me for the third time in five minutes. Good thing the neighbors started arriving before she could get too mushy.

"Family Reunion" by the O'Jays roared through the speakers, welcoming everyone to the party. They hugged and greeted each other like the old days. Even Ms. Elise seemed like her usual self. Smiles jumped from one face to the next. Jas's plan to mix up the food stations worked perfectly. This was the happiest I'd seen my neighbors in weeks.

After we ate, it was time for dancing. Jas was the official deejay.

Brent led the *Soul Train* line. He jumped right up front with no hesitation *and* no permission. It was kinda weird having him act like things were normal between us. Brent has always been good at staying cool even if things aren't going as well as they look. To him, maybe, things were normal, but to me things were all messed up.

Brent bounced and slid down the *Soul Train* line with neighbors on both sides cheering him on. Mr. and Mrs. Williams jumped right up, shimmying down the line after him. Kari was too shy to dance, so he just walked down the line high-fiving everyone. Mom and Dad made their way to the front, bumping hips as they danced down the line. Alyssa and I were next. We'd ended up wearing the same camo-patterned Chucks—we were the best dressed and had the best moves.

Next up was the Wobble. When the song started, everyone found a spot with enough space to dance. "Wobble Baby" blasted through the speaker. We jumped forward, jumped backward, twisted, and wobbled to the beat. Kari even joined in. After three full rotations, the crowd was bumping into each other and turning in different directions.

Before Brent could start another round of the Wobble, Kari started the slideshow. Everyone watched in amazement as the pictures flipped.

Slide: The summer the water main broke and flooded the streets, Brent surfed down the block in his underwear.

Slide: Jas practicing his talent show drum solo on the Silvas' front porch. He won first place that year.

Slide: Alyssa's mom, Ms. Watkins, won Yard of the Month for her flower bed, a tradition that ended after she won twelve months in a row.

Slide: Mr. Hank dressed in seventies clothes—complete with a huge Afro—from his old-school birthday party a few years ago.

Slide: Last summer when everybody helped repave the brick walkway near the fountain in the park.

After the last slide flipped, tears streamed down the faces of many of the neighbors. It was like a warm blanket, fresh out of the dryer, was wrapped around the park.

Alyssa nudged me, letting me know it was time. I made my way to the front of the crowd and peered out at everyone. Speaking to everyone in the neighborhood was the last thing I wanted to do. Mom had helped me write what I wanted to say, and it wasn't as bad as talking to a news camera, but still bad enough. And suddenly my shirt felt too tight—I yanked on the collar a little. It didn't help.

I looked down at the ground and took a deep breath. That didn't help either, and now my stomach was playing Twister. When I lifted my head, smiling, happy faces looked back at me. Mr. Baker gave me the nod.

"Thank y'all for coming. It's cool to see everyone getting along." A few chuckles from the crowd let me know they got my joke. "We want to thank Ms. Baker and Mr. Monica . . . I mean, Mr. Baker and Ms. Monica, and Save Our City for helping us. I hope this reminds everybody of the happy times we've had in the Oaks."

Just a few more lines.

"I represent the second generation of my family to grow up here. My grandpa worked hard saving money so he could one day own a home in this neighborhood. I'm sure all of you did too, and I think that's worth fighting for." I looked over at Mom; she was giving me a thumbs-up from her spot right at the front. "Thank you, that's all."

Alyssa's smile meant I'd done a good job, even though it felt like my stomach had climbed into my throat. I wasn't sure if the block party would convince everyone to reject the offer from Simmons Development Group, but it felt like we were a community again—smiling and talking and hugging—and I never wanted that feeling to end.

When the party was over, it was time to help clean up.

"Kari, Wes, you guys go get the wheelbarrows from my backyard. We'll need something to wheel this trash over to the dumpsters," Mr. Hank said.

Kari and I ran over to Mr. Hank's house and into the backyard. We were on our way back to the park when the *chirp* of a siren stopped us in our tracks.

"Aaay, boys, where y'all takin' them barrows to?"

We turned to find a police officer yelling from his patrol car. He didn't look familiar. I thought I knew all the police officers who patrolled Kensington Oaks.

"Y'all hear me?" the officer yelled.

"Yes sir, we're taking them to the park," Kari answered.

"Wrong. The right answer is nowhere," the officer said. "Where you live, boy?"

He was talking to Kari but looking at me—then at Kari.

"I used to live here, but now I live off Martin Luther King Jr. Boulevard. My friend lives across the street, though."

My mouth was superglued shut. That stomach-in-throat thing was happening again.

Kari gave me a quick nudge.

"Ugh . . . yes sir, I live across the street," I said. My voice was so small I could barely hear it myself.

"Looks like y'all are trespassin'."

Before we could say anything else, the officer jumped out of his car.

"Lay on the ground!" he screamed.

Kari and I dropped the wheelbarrows and dove to the pavement.

I lay there frozen, afraid to move. The sidewalk was hard and rough against my skin. I couldn't believe this was happening. I tried to play back the past few moments, but my mind kept warping the tape. *Don't talk back. Say* yes sir. *Do as you are told.* All I could think of were Dad's words. We'd had this talk more than once. My only job was to make it home.

"We didn't do nothing!" Kari yelled, his face pressed against the pavement.

"*Shut up!* In fact—you with the nappy hair—come with me!" the officer howled at Kari. Then he pointed at me. "You, get up and tell this one's parents he'll be at the station on Montford."

"Wait!" I called out. But it was too late. The officer had thrown Kari into the back seat of the police car.

15

I sprinted back to the park. Tears rimmed my eyes. My vision was blurry and crossed.

"Wes! What's wrong?" Mom asked.

"Mom, he took Kari!" I fought my tired lungs for every word.

"Who took Kari?" Dad asked.

"The policeman. He just grabbed him."

"Why, what happened?" Dad asked.

"We were getting the wheelbarrows and he stopped us. Said we were trespassing. He made us get on the ground," I said, bent over, panting. "Kari told him we weren't doing anything wrong. And that was it. He threw Kari in the back seat."

Mom grabbed me and pulled me close to her chest. "Was it an officer you know?" she asked, rubbing her hands through my hair.

"No, I've never seen him before."

"Let's go get Kari," Dad said, marching away from the park toward our house.

"He took him to Montford," I said, following behind.

"Why Montford? That's not even our precinct."

Me, Mom, Dad, and Mr. Hank jumped in the SUV and headed to the police station.

■ ■ ■

I had only been in a police station one time in my life. It was for a class field trip. As we walked inside, I instantly remembered the stale gray walls and the smell of old coffee.

The small station was filled with mismatched people. There was a man sleeping on a bench near the doorway, his shoes tossed on the floor. An older lady who looked like someone's grandmother sat quietly in a corner near the bathroom. Her clothes were filthy and torn. The dirt smudged on her face said she hadn't had a bath in weeks. She seemed to be in her own world, like she wasn't even there. She only glanced up when an officer rushed past us, herding in two teen boys not much older than me.

The hair on my arms stood up. I moved closer to Mom. This place was creepy.

The waiting area was in a corner right past the front desk. Mom and I found a seat while Dad and Mr. Hank stood in line. There were three people ahead of them.

"Why would the police bring Kari here?" I asked Mom.

"This station is closer to where Kari lives."

"Do you think he'll get arrested?"

"No, Wes, this is just a misunderstanding." Mom seemed calmer now, which made me feel a little better.

It was Dad's turn at the desk. I couldn't hear what he was saying, but his face said it all. Total seriousness, no humor. Dad didn't get angry often, but right now he had fire in his eyes. I'd been on the other side of that look before, and I was glad it wasn't me this time.

The intensity in Dad's walk was hard enough to shake the floor. He closed the gap from the desk to the waiting area in three steps. Mr. Hank walked behind him.

"Everything is fine. Kari will be released shortly," Dad said.

"Why did the officer bring him here, anyway? He didn't do anything," I said.

"Officer Stewart said Kari was wandering around in a neighborhood he didn't live in. He claims he decided to give Kari a ride home, but Kari wouldn't tell him where he lived. So they stopped at the station to call his mom and get his address." Dad had a heavy dose of "yeah right" in his voice.

"He wasn't wandering," I said. "And he pushed Kari into the car."

"I told them I sent you both to get the wheelbarrows from my backyard," Mr. Hank added.

Heat rushed through my veins. It didn't matter where Kari lived—the officer had no right to take him.

We waited another hour before Officer Stewart brought Kari from the back room. The officer was shorter than I thought; in fact, he was only a few inches taller than Kari. He had a round stomach and a balding head. He'd felt like a giant standing over us, just hours earlier. I stared into his eyes; they were dull and mean.

Most of the officers who patrol the Oaks are Black. They all know me and Kari. Officer Stewart was white, and he apparently knew nothing about the Oaks and who lived there. Kari and his family had only moved away a couple years ago.

"I spoke to his momma. She said it was fine to release this fella to a Walter Henderson," Officer Stewart said.

"That's me," Dad said. "Are you okay, Kari?"

"Yes sir." Kari's voice was barely above a whisper. His eyes were red and glossy. "My mom is still at work, but she said it's okay for me to stay the night at your house."

"Okay, let's go home," Mom said, wrapping her arm around Kari.

■ ■ ■

When we got back home, I thought Mom and Dad would be full of advice for what Kari and I should have done differently. Instead, Dad kept asking if we were okay. Mom kept hugging us—and we let her.

"Is there anything you boys want to ask us about what happened tonight?" Dad asked.

"Why didn't the officer take me too?" I asked.

"I don't know, Wes. He said that you live in this neighborhood and Kari doesn't."

"He didn't give me a chance to explain that I used to live here too. He just pushed me into the car. It was like he didn't even hear me talking," Kari said. "Like someone turned my voice off."

I could tell Dad was thinking about what to say next. He always has the right answers, but this was different—like he was searching in a puzzle box for the right piece.

"Kari, I think we have grounds to file a complaint against Officer Stewart," Dad said finally. "I want you to think about if that's something you'd like to do."

"Will that stop him from doing this again?" Kari asked.

"There's no guarantee, but you can use your voice to fight against what happened to you," Dad said.

"I think I want to do it," Kari said.

"Let's talk more in the morning," Mom said.

"Today was a hard day—you both did good. Now let's try to get some sleep," Dad said.

We said good night and Dad flicked off the light and closed the door behind him. Kari and I usually slept with our heads at opposite ends of my full-sized bed. Tonight we collapsed side by side in the same direction.

You with the nappy hair—come with me. . . . Officer Stewart's words kept playing over and over in my mind. The thing is, I see the officers who patrol the Oaks all the time. Sometimes they get on us neighborhood kids for playing in the street or for throwing trash on the ground, but nothing serious.

This one officer—who used to live across the street from Jas—would pay us to wash his police car during the summer. He even came back to help with the block party last year.

The only time I ever played on a football team was with the Police Activities League. I'm no good at football, but it was fun having the officers as coaches. And when I twisted my ankle halfway into the season, Officer Jefferies made sure I got a participation trophy even though I participated the least.

I never thought the police killings from TV that Mom made me march for had anything to do with the Oaks. But the way Officer Stewart had stood over us, ordering us around when we hadn't done anything wrong, made me think about how bad things could happen even when you're trying to do good.

16

At school on Monday, word traveled fast about Officer Stewart forcing Kari into his police car. That's one of the bad things about having a close community. Everybody knows everybody's business. Apparently, my neighbor Mrs. York saw Kari in the back seat of the police car as it drove away. After a string of text messages and phone calls, the word was out.

Kari hadn't talked much about it. Actually, for all I knew he hadn't said anything at all after leaving our house the next day. I knew how scared he must have been, but he kept it all bottled up inside. The image of him exploding was what made me worry. Kinda like a bottle of soda shaken over and over, then *POP!*—an explosion.

Everyone rallied around Kari to show support, everyone except Mya. Mya was being even more Mya than she usually was.

"I heard the block party didn't turn out so great," she said. The glare in her eyes brimmed with mean.

"Actually, it turned out pretty awesome. You should've come," I said.

"It turned out pretty awesome? Right. When? Before Kari went and got himself arrested?"

"Kari wasn't arrested, and that police officer was wrong, not Kari," I said, narrowing my eyes. "I can't believe you're letting one stupid joke from a long time ago come between you and Kari. We used to all be best friends."

"Look, Wes, things change," Mya said, putting her hands on her hips. "And with all the changes going on around here, I need to tell you something. My dad bringing me all the way to the Grove isn't working out. He only agreed to let me go to school here because I promised him I would stay out of trouble and keep my grades up, and that was only a two-month trial. That trial didn't include planning parties or having my friends—or used-to-be-friend—get arrested."

I knew Mya didn't like hanging with us like she used to, but I never expected her to act like this.

Mya continued, "So this week is my last week at the Grove. It makes more sense for me to go to the middle school closest to my house."

Instead of going back and forth with Mya, I walked away. I'd tried to stay out of this mess with her and Kari, but this time I needed to be there for him.

17

These past few days had been the longest. I'd spent most of it trying to forget about the police stopping Kari and my fight with Mya. I'd finally chosen climate change as my topic (I stole that idea from Brent) for the fall project, but I hadn't even started on the paper yet.

Instead of waiting for Mom to wake me up the next morning, I rolled out of bed and headed to the park before school to shoot hoops. I needed something, *anything,* to clear my head. I grabbed my good ball and worked on my handles on the short walk over to the park. The pulse from the ball bouncing against the beat-up pavement vibrated through me—the rhythm giving me energy.

I was practicing free throws when Dad walked up.

"Clearing your mind?" he asked.

"Yeah, I guess," I said. I was glad Dad didn't press me to say any more. He fell in beside me, shooting a couple free throws to get warmed up. Then we played a quick game of one-on-one.

I still wasn't able to beat Dad, but I *did* make him break a sweat. I was a whole foot shorter, making it a little difficult to block Dad's shot, but what I lacked in size I made up for in effort, and I had quick hands.

"It's time to clean up and get to school," Dad said as he sank the winning basket.

"I'm gonna beat you one day," I said, running to grab the rebound.

"One day maybe, but not today," Dad said, laughing.

■ ■ ■

All the energy from that morning dripped out of my fingers and crept down the hall when I crossed the doorway into Ms. Hardy's class.

The thing I dreaded most about Ms. Hardy's class was having my quiz paper returned. She had this painful ritual where she walked the papers around to each student. She passed out the good grades first, the so-so grades next, and the bad grades last. I didn't think that was fair. Yes, maybe I *should* get better grades, but that was my business and no one else's.

I slumped into my seat behind Alyssa and waited.

"Good morning, class," Ms. Hardy started. "Please direct your attention to the front of the classroom. Today we'll be going over the quiz you took last week." A rumble of grunts shook the room as soon as the word *quiz* escaped her lips. "Ahem, like I said, we will be reviewing the quiz." Ms. Hardy raised her voice to speak over the rumbles. "I'm proud to say we had three students with a perfect score!"

I knew one of those three was Alyssa. She had the highest grade in the class, and she always got her quiz paper returned first. She'd probably grow up to be a mathematician or maybe even one of those super-smart computer programmers. Ms. Hardy said girls are taking the tech world by storm. Yeah, I could see Alyssa doing that.

Ms. Hardy smiled as she handed Alyssa her quiz. I peeked around Alyssa's braided ponytail to see a bright pink $A++$ written at the top of her paper. I waited for my turn. Ms. Hardy made her way from one side of the room to the other, handing out papers. As her stack got thinner and thinner, I knew I wasn't in the so-so group this time.

When she finally stopped in front of me, she had four papers left. Three kids had done worse than I had. I cringed when I saw the huge red D at the top of my paper. I tucked it into my folder before anyone else could see it.

When will I ever need to know the volume and surface area of a rectangular prism, anyway?

Ms. Hardy went over the quiz, question by question, reworking each problem. She said she would let the kids with low grades turn in extra credit to improve their score *if* we brought the quiz back to her initialed by a parent. I had another lecture coming.

I was on my way to lunch when Kari stopped me in the hallway.

"Wes, I need your help," he said. I didn't know what was wrong, but I could tell by the look in his eyes that it couldn't be good.

"Wassup, Kari? You okay?"

"My mom made her mind up. She says we have to move to my aunt's house."

"What? When?" Dang, I couldn't believe Kari was gonna have to move again.

"In two weeks."

"Why now?"

"After the thing happened with the police, we keep getting patrol cars riding past the hotel. The guys around the way let it be known that they don't like the extra attention. I don't think the police are after me, but it could start trouble for the other guys. I told my mom we should file a complaint, like your dad said. But she thinks that would get me into more trouble."

"But the officer was wrong," I said.

"I know! That's what I told Mom. She said it's best if we leave town, though. She already wanted to, and now with all these new police officers starting trouble, she doesn't want to wait."

Maybe Ms. Tasha was right. Getting Kari away from the hotel could be a good thing.

But what if he didn't have to move all the way to his aunt's? This could be a way for me to make it up to him for not being there this summer.

"Maybe you can stay with us for a while. I'm sure my mom and dad would be fine with it." I wasn't *sure* sure, but pretty sure—I mean, Kari had always stayed nights at our house, especially when things were going down between his parents. This was kinda like the same thing.

"You think they'll let me?"

"Of course they will." At least I hoped so. Mom and Dad are all about helping people, and Dad had said himself that he missed Kari being around.

That afternoon, when the last bell rang, me and Kari met up in the courtyard. We would get the okay and move Kari's things that night. We planned to present our idea at dinner.

When Mom started to scoop chicken potpie onto my plate, I gave Kari the nod.

He wasted no time starting the conversation. "I talked to my mom about filing the complaint with the police department. She said it was a bad idea."

That really got Dad's attention, 'cause he even put his fork down and turned toward Kari. "Did she say why?" Dad asked.

"She said it would only make the officer madder."

"Well, Kari, you have to respect your mother's decision," Dad said. That definitely meant he didn't agree.

"She also said we'd be better off moving out of town for a while," Kari continued. "She's worried about Danica."

"So Kari can stay with us, right?" I asked, turning to Dad.

"Wait a minute, Wes," Dad said, pushing his chair back from the table.

"There's no reason for Kari to leave. Ms. Tasha and Danica can go, and he can stay with us," I went on. "He's had to move enough times already."

"Wes, hold on," Mom said. "That's not a decision we can make so easily."

"There are lots of things to consider, and we would need to talk to Tasha," Dad said. "Kari, when does your mom want to leave?"

"In two weeks."

"For how long?" Dad asked.

"I don't know. She said maybe till the summer . . ." Kari's voice trailed off and he looked over at me.

I had to do something. "See, Dad, Kari can stay here and live in the Oaks again," I said. "None of this of Kari's fault, and he shouldn't have to move."

"Of course none of this is Kari's fault. But, Wes, your mom and I need some time to think about this." Dad's voice was plain—no sugar.

"But why? You always say how much you miss Kari, and he used to stay over all the time, and he won't have to deal with all the stuff happening at the hotel," I said. "Mom? What do you think?"

"Wes, listen to your father. He and I need to talk about this."

I could feel my face getting hot. I leaned back in my chair, trying to think of something else that might convince Dad to let Kari stay with us. This was supposed to be easy, but we weren't speaking the same language. Dad was Charlie Brown's teacher and all I heard was *wah wah wah wah wah wah*. And all this time I thought Mom was the hardest to convince.

"Look, Kari, Maxine and I love you. You've been like a second child to us, but the fact of the matter is, you have a family. We aren't saying no, but we do need to think about all the facts and talk to your mother," Dad continued. *Wah wah wah wah wah wah*.

"Yes sir," Kari mumbled.

My fork clanked against my plate as I stabbed peas and pieces of carrot, separating the veggies from the rest of the potpie. Every time I thought of a new point to add, I stopped myself. All this chanting and marching for other people and we could actually do something to help Kari—right here, right now!

18

Instead of going home the next day after school, I stopped at Jas's house. I didn't feel comfortable escaping to Brent's house the way I used to. His family was still thinking about leaving the Oaks, and he was acting funny about me and Mr. Baker. Plus, I knew Mr. and Mrs. Silva wouldn't mind me crashing for dinner. The vibe was cooler at Jas's than at my house, anyway, and the last thing I wanted to do was sit in the house with my parents, staring at the walls or watching the news.

Jas lives four streets over from me. The houses on his street are identical to mine, but the neighbors on Jas's street are newer to the Oaks. Brent calls it Little Mexico, which doesn't make sense, because only three Mexican families live on the block. The Silvas are from Brazil.

I could see the sunny yellow walls of the Silvas' living room from the yard. Their front door is always open when they're home. I walked up onto the porch and knocked on the door, even though I could see Mr. Silva on the couch staring at the TV.

"Come on in, Wes, it's open," Mr. Silva said. "Jasper's

back in his room, with that noise going. Go ahead back there."

I slipped my shoes off and scooted past Mr. Silva, who was sunk down into the bright orange couch. A collection of yellow, orange, and blue pillows framed him. The rug beneath his feet was a picture of a tropical sunset. The swirls of pink and orange met a sea of blue. It was almost too pretty to put your feet on. I guess that's why no one wears shoes in the Silvas' house.

"Jas!" I called out as I turned the corner.

"Hey, Wes, I didn't know you were stopping by. You eating with us?"

"You think your mom will be cool with it?"

"You know it."

"Good, my parents trippin' and I'm trying not to go home yet."

"All good, man."

Jas isn't the kind to get all up in someone's business, so he didn't ask any more questions. He just flipped through the channels on the TV while the speakers mounted on his wall blared. I don't see much point in watching TV *and* listening to music, but Jas always has music playing in his room—through his speakers or earbuds, sometimes both at the same time. The bass was pumping so loud we barely heard Mrs. Silva call us to dinner.

"Go ahead and start without me," Mr. Silva called from the living room. He always eats on the couch in front of the TV—that's that cool vibe you'd never find at my house.

"Thanks, Mrs. Silva, everything smells really good," I said. I grabbed a seat at the table across from Jas.

"Thanks, Wes. Your mom called—she said it was okay for you to stay for dinner."

I glanced at Jas. "Oh, she did?" I said under my breath. Jas shrugged and dug his fork into his dish of feijoada, made with black beans and sausage. Mrs. Silva makes the most awesome food, food I only get to eat at their house. Feijoada is one of my favorites, and brigadeiro. I love brigadeiro.

"So, Wes, how's school going?" Mrs. Silva asked.

"Hope your grades are better than Jasper's!" Mr. Silva called from his spot on the couch.

Jas stuck his tongue out in the direction of the living room. I laughed and turned to Mrs. Silva and said, "It's going okay. It's not much different from Oak Gardens." That was a lie, but it sounded better than complaining about the D I'd gotten on my math quiz or how long it had taken me to decide on my topic for the fall social studies project.

I looked up at the parrot-shaped clock on the wall in the kitchen: 7:38 p.m. I knew Mom would kill me if

I didn't get home soon. I finished my last scoop of rice, thanked Mrs. Silva, and headed out the door.

The walk home was like being summoned to the principal's office. I hadn't really spoken to Mom and Dad since the night before, when Dad had pretty much shut down my idea of Kari staying with us for a while. I tiptoed onto the porch and turned the knob of the front door—it was unlocked. I pushed the door lightly and peeked into the living room—all clear. I crept across the room, down the hall, and into my bedroom—safe.

Before I could close the door, Dad appeared in the doorway. "First and last time you aren't home for dinner without permission."

I looked at the floor and nodded.

"And Ms. Hardy emailed your mom and me to make sure you were getting all the help you need in math. When were you going to tell us about your quiz grade?" Dad continued.

"I . . . ," I started.

"No TV and no video games until the extra credit assignment is complete. Do I make myself clear?" Dad said. No sugar.

"Yes sir," I whispered. And just like that, I had a new problem to deal with.

■ ■ ■

Mom had marked a big X on the calendar in the kitchen for today's date. The X meant today was the last day of the sixty-day offer period from Simmons. It had come and gone with no fuss at all. After the block party, almost all our neighbors had decided to hold out on accepting the offer. It seemed like everything was moving right along with the plan to stop Simmons Development Group. Which felt like the only good thing going on these days, but it was a big good thing, almost big enough to forget about everything else. A little happy bubble floated over me by the time I met with Jas, Alyssa, Kari, and Mr. Baker after school.

"We did it!" I said, giving everybody a pound.

"The Oaks is safe. Right?" asked Jas.

"Let's hope so," Mr. Baker said.

I could tell Mr. Baker wasn't so sure this was the end of the fight, but I was relieved. Everything in the Oaks seemed good again. I dismissed the meeting and headed home.

"Hey, Wes, wait up," Kari said, running to catch up. "Have your parents said anything about me coming to live with you guys?"

"Nope, nothing. Sorry, Kari." I had gotten Kari overhyped about moving in with us, but I should've known better than to rush my parents. When they said wait, they meant it. The other day, this really had seemed like something I could actually fix, but it was turning out to be harder than I thought it would be.

Since my NBA 2K battle with Jas after the meeting was a no-go, I decided to help Mom with dinner. Maybe I could convince her to make up her mind.

"Who are you, and what have you done with my son?" Mom asked.

"Moooom . . . really."

"Okay, you can chop the potatoes," she said, handing me a knife.

My knife banged against the cutting board as I pressed it into the potatoes. I wasn't sure if I should bring up Kari or wait for Mom to. So I waited.

After a few moments Mom said, "Wes, I know you're worried, but we haven't forgotten about Kari. Your dad and I will have an answer sometime this week, but I want you to think about this too."

"I have," I said. "I want to help Kari."

"But why are you so certain Kari living with us will help him? There are other ways to help Kari."

Kari needed somewhere to live—what was so difficult about that? I wasn't there for him when he was forced out of the apartment building; I needed to be there for him now.

"Yeah, but if he moves, he'll have to go to another school. You know how hard it is for him to make new friends," I said finally.

"I understand, but, Wes, you need to think about how this will impact us. Having another person in the house will affect the time we spend together."

"Okay, Mom, I'll think about it," I said, dropping my shoulders.

Maybe Mom was right. I had my parents all to myself. When I was younger, I always asked why I was an only child. Mom and Dad would just say that was God's plan for our family. It was only last year that I learned Mom *couldn't* have another child. Something bad had happened when I was born; the doctors said she couldn't have any more kids. I'm Mom's special gift.

I wanted Kari to feel special too. After Kari's parents divorced and his dad stopped coming around, he had to become the man at his house. Ms. Tasha depended on Kari to help with everything. Kari told me once, "I have to step up now." Which didn't seem fair, since his parents were the ones who decided to get a divorce. His dad should be the one stepping up, or at least showing up. Living with us would give Kari a chance to be a regular kid again.

I was setting the table for dinner when Dad got home from work.

Before he could lay his oily uniform shirt on the couch, Mom's eyes shot toward the laundry basket. Dad laughed and tossed his shirt into the basket.

"Hey, son. Are you actually helping with dinner?"

"Daaad!"

"I'm impressed, that's all," Dad teased.

As we sat down to dinner, I noticed a package delivery truck stop in front of the house.

"I'll get it," I said, hopping up and opening the front door.

All those feelings of relief from earlier in the day dissolved when I saw SIMMONS DEVELOPMENT GROUP typed on the large envelope.

This couldn't be good news. I wished I could throw it away.

"Wes, what is it?" Dad asked.

I dropped the envelope in his hand.

"Hmmm, let's see what they've come up with now," Dad said.

"Let's eat dinner first. Wes and I prepared an awesome meal. We can deal with that later," Mom said, shooing the envelope away like it was a stray cat.

I ate dinner, but I didn't taste a thing. I might as well have been eating cardboard. I barely responded to the normal questioning by Mom and Dad. All I could think about was the envelope. SIMMONS DEVELOPMENT GROUP was seared onto the inside of my eyelids.

After dinner was done and the kitchen cleaned, Dad sat down to open the envelope. Inside were a letter and several drawings.

"Simmons would like to meet with each home-owner again to make another offer," Dad said. He read a portion of the letter aloud: "'We realize our original offer was grossly undervalued and would like to meet to discuss a more appropriate figure. . . . Please see the enclosed drawings of the redevelopment plans.'"

"Looks like we need to gear up for round two," Mom said to Dad.

"I'm ready!" I said, jumping up from my seat.

"Wes, you've done a lot to help, but we're tagging you out," Mom said.

"Mom . . ."

"This second offer makes things more serious. It's time for the adults to take this over," Mom said. "Not to mention, you have extra math assignments to finish. And have you finished your social studies project?"

"I picked a topic, but—"

"We mean it, Wesley. School is your first priority. You're done with this," Dad said, leveling me with a laser stare.

I nodded, but I didn't intend to bow out now. There was no way I was backing down.

19

The community board called an emergency meeting about the second offer the next day. The yelling and screaming started the moment everyone piled into the community center. No one even bothered to sit down.

This was the worst meeting yet. I was supposed to be working on my fall project, but I had to see what was going on. I'd snuck in the back door after everyone arrived. I almost wished I hadn't. I stood quietly in the back of the room so Mom wouldn't see me. I watched my neighbors fight with each other like whiny babies.

"Listen to me . . ."

"I'm done listening . . ."

"Everyone be quiet!"

Harsh words and sharp tones spun around me like a tornado. Louder and louder. The yelling clouded my head. I planted my feet on the ground to steady myself. I couldn't take another moment of this. I darted out the back door.

The crisp fall air cooled my face.

"You okay, Wes?"

I turned to see Alyssa standing there; her shining

eyes brightened the cloud around me. I hadn't seen her inside the community center. I tried to check her out without staring. She was wearing a gray-and-white polka-dotted bubble vest, a denim skirt, and gray leggings. Her black furry boots reached just up to her knees. Her hair was braided back halfway, the rest loose in fluffy curls.

"Yeah, I'm okay," I said.

"Can you believe how everyone's acting?"

"No. It's a mess."

"I don't know if we can fix this," Alyssa said.

"Me either."

For the first time, I allowed myself to think about what would happen if me and my family had to leave Kensington Oaks. *Would we end up like Kari? Living in a hotel? Or moving all the way to the suburbs like my cousins?* My eyes started to fill with tears. Alyssa walked over and wrapped her arms around me. I wrapped my arms back around her and held on tight.

Tears dripped down Alyssa's cheeks.

"It's okay. We'll find a way to make this better," I said.

I didn't believe my own words, but I hoped saying them aloud would make them more true. Alyssa took a couple steps back and smoothed out her skirt. I reached up to wipe her tears away. Her lips curled into a half smile.

"Y'all doing okay out here?" Mr. Hank said.

I jumped back, stumbling over a rock on the ground.

"Yes, yes, she's fine, I mean, we're fine . . . I mean good," I said, fumbling over my words.

"I know things got a little out of control in there, but we'll work it out. Don't y'all worry," Mr. Hank said.

I was tired of people telling me not to worry.

■ ■ ■

The next week at school was like being force-fed cold oatmeal. I'd finished my extra math assignments and turned in the opening paragraph for my fall social studies report. Mr. Baker had said he wanted to check our progress—I think he wanted to make sure we hadn't picked boring topics.

I'd spent a few afternoons in the school's library trying to work on the rest of my report. But with everything I'd read, I still didn't understand all the science behind climate change, and we were years behind on slowing down the effects. I didn't really want to dump all that bad news in my report. As I settled in at my normal table in the back corner of the library, I spotted Ms. Monica talking to the school librarian. Kinda weird that she'd be here, since we'd stopped the meetings in Mr. Baker's room.

She was wearing navy pants with lavender pinstripes.

The pinstripes were a perfect match to her lavender top. Her metallic pointy-toe heels poked out under her pant cuffs.

"Hey, Ms. Monica," I said, walking over to her.

"Hi, Wesley. How are things going in Kensington Oaks?"

"Not good." I didn't even know where to start. "Simmons made new offers worth a bunch more money. A lot of families want to accept. Everyone is fighting again. The Oaks doesn't even feel like home anymore."

"I see."

"I don't know what else to do. If they want to accept the offers, I guess I should stop fighting and let them." I thought about all the yelling at the last meeting and about Kari and my parents. And Ms. Tasha making Kari move again. What was the point of arguing? It seemed like the adults were going to do what they wanted to do anyway.

"I understand how you feel, but you've had too many successes to give up now. Sometimes change takes a long time," Ms. Monica said. "'The arc of the moral universe is long, but it bends toward justice.'"

I thought I'd heard Mom say that before, and I was pretty sure it meant Ms. Monica wasn't about to let me give up. "What else can I do?" I asked.

"You'll have to get a bit more creative. Research some other options," she said. "I'll be thinking too, and if you find something I can help with, please let me know."

"Okay." I wasn't very encouraged. It seemed like everything was harder than it was supposed to be.

On my walk home from school, I stopped in the park. Just weeks ago, the park shone with laughter and light from the block party, but today all I saw was darkness.

My favorite spot in the park is the brick path that leads from the long row of oak trees. At the very end of the path is an old water fountain. It's about three feet tall with a small steel water basin, and carved into its base is a row of swirly leaves.

Last year when the community repaved the walkway, the board debated getting rid of the fountain, but I was glad they'd decided to keep it. I've always felt a connection to it; whenever me and my friends used to play hide-and-seek, I would take off running toward the fountain. If I arrived there untouched, I knew I'd made it safely home.

I left the park wondering if anyone else even cared about the Oaks as much as I did. Mom, Dad, and Mr. Hank probably did, but most of my other neighbors only seemed to care about money.

When I got home, Mom and Dad were there waiting on me.

"Hey, Dad, you're home early." My insides got all

queasy like when we first found out about the offer letter. I knew something was up.

"Hey, son. Your mom and I want to talk to you about something."

"Okay . . ."

"We just got off the phone with Kari and his mom. We've decided now isn't the right time for Kari to move in with us. And Tasha agreed."

My heart dropped to my toes. "Why not?"

"Our future in Kensington Oaks is in jeopardy. The last thing we want is for Kari to move in and have to face more instability if we get forced out too."

"But can't he finish the school year at the Grove?"

"At this point we aren't even sure *you'll* finish this year at the Grove. We have to start seriously thinking about the possibility of living somewhere else." No sugar.

"Can I go to my room?" I didn't even wait on an answer. I marched down the hall and closed my bedroom door. I couldn't handle any more bad news.

20

The skies poured buckets of rain on Kari's last day at the Grove. I guess the heavens were crying, since no one else seemed to care that Kari was leaving. Kari didn't even seem to care himself. I knew it was an act, though. He cared; he just wasn't good at showing it.

Kari hadn't told anyone except Jas and Alyssa he'd be leaving. I figured he didn't want to deal with the questions from anyone else. He got straight to the point. "So, my mom is moving us to live with my aunt. Tomorrow is my last day," he'd said after school the day before.

"Oh no! Why?" Alyssa had asked. She looked shocked.

"Things not going too good where we live now," Kari had said.

"Why can't you stay till Friday?" Jas asked.

"Tomorrow is the only day my uncle can move us."

I had wondered the same thing. Why would Ms. Tasha make them move on a Wednesday? A stupid Wednesday, in the middle of the week?

Kari had started eating lunch at our table since Mya wasn't around anymore. Now today would be our last lunch together—our last day together, period. Alyssa, Jas, Kari, and I filed into the café and settled at our regular table, though not much eating or talking was going on. Alyssa had brought Kari some peanut butter M&M's; they were his favorite. She said they were his going-away present. Kari actually cracked a smile when she gave them to him. It only lasted a few seconds, but I saw it.

"Why y'all look so mad?" Brent said when he joined us in the café. He slung his wet book bag off his shoulder and onto the lunch table, splashing water on everyone.

Jas looked at Alyssa, Alyssa looked at me, and I looked at Kari. Finally, Kari answered, "Today is my last day."

"You for real?"

"Yeah," Kari sighed.

"Dang, you moving again?" Brent asked. Alyssa shot him a look of death. "What?" he mouthed to Alyssa.

"Yep, moving again," Kari answered.

"Well, we're going to miss you," Brent said, reaching over to dap Kari.

"Yes, we'll all miss you," Alyssa said.

Random chatter and the sound of rain dancing on the windows filled the café during the rest of the lunch period, but there was only silence at our table. There was nothing left to say.

When the last bell rang for the day, I ran to catch up with Kari at his locker. I was glad it was just the two of us. Kari stacked his textbooks into one corner of the locker while he packed the other things into his bag.

I rocked back and forth from one foot to the other, trying to think of the right words. "I'm gonna keep talking to my mom and dad about you moving in with us. They'll give in, I know it," I said.

"Okay," Kari said. He didn't believe me. He tossed his bag over his shoulder. "Well, I gotta go. My mom is picking me up from school and we're going straight there."

"Oh, okay . . . well . . . see you later. . . ."

"Bye," Kari said, reaching over to give me a half hug.

I watched him walk down the corridor. "Bye," I said to myself.

I felt tears coming, but I brushed them away. If Kari wasn't crying, I wouldn't cry either.

21

It had been almost three weeks since Kari left. I needed something to get my mood up. That something was Halloween. It was my second-favorite holiday—behind Christmas, of course. The only person I knew who loved Halloween more than me was Mya. She came up with our group costume idea every year. It took her weeks to pick the perfect theme, and when she was ready, she presented her costume designs to us on her tablet complete with colored sketches.

Mya's neighborhood also had a huge Halloween party in their clubhouse. One of the highlights of the party was a costume contest—the best costume won a trophy. Mya had won the kids' category two years in a row, and our crew had won Best Group Costume just as many times.

Last year, we went as superheroes at a wedding. We wore regular superhero outfits but added dress-up clothes on top to make them look fancy. Then during the costume judging, we ripped off the dressy top layer and blew their minds. We won hands down.

The other awesome thing about Halloween in Mya's

neighborhood was the candy. People in rich neighbor-hoods give *the best* treats—I'm talking full-sized candy bars. One time I even got a king-sized pack of Reese's cups.

"Wes, can you and Mya please make up so we can go to the costume party?" Jas asked me for the third time that day.

We were at my house eating pizza, waiting for it to get dark enough to go trick-or-treating.

"Think about how weak tricking-or-treating in the Oaks is compared to Mya's neighborhood," Brent said. "You're trippin'."

"Can we at least see if Alyssa is going with Mya?" Jas asked.

"I told you she is. I asked her in homeroom this morning," I said.

"Maybe she'll stash away some candy for us," Brent said.

"That's a good idea," Jas said. "Let's go ask her."

They both grabbed a slice of pizza and headed for the door. I trailed behind them down the block to Alyssa's house.

We looked like a bunch of misfits in our last-minute costumes. Jas wore his band uniform, including that stupid hat. I was dressed as Steph Curry—I already had the jersey and shoes; I just added some basketball shorts and colored on a fake beard. Brent was dressed as Brent.

He wore the same clothes he'd had on at school earlier that day. Even though Mya could be annoying, we were a mess without her.

"Are y'all really wearing regular clothes for Halloween?" Alyssa asked when she saw us. She was decked out in a glittery zombie outfit. I'm sure she and Mya had something special planned, but I was too salty to ask what.

"This is all Wes's fault! Please take us with you," Jas pleaded.

"Man, y'all just gonna leave me?" I said, looking at Jas and Brent.

"Nah, if Mya didn't invite us we'll stay here . . . with you . . . but, Alyssa, can you pleeeease bring us back some candy?" Brent said, with his palms pressed together like praying hands.

"I'll see what I can do," Alyssa said.

She probably felt sorry for them like I did. I mean, it wasn't really their fault we weren't invited. After our argument, Mya had stopped talking to everyone in the crew except for Alyssa. Everybody expected me to fix it—but it wasn't my fault either.

We left Alyssa's house and waited in the park until it was dark enough to start knocking on doors. I wished I could push time forward, because I was tired of being ripped on by Brent and I was ready to just get this over with.

When the sun was down, we started our trek around the Oaks.

It was just as boring as Brent said it would be. Half the houses had their lights off, and one guy was wack enough to give out those square orange peanut butter crackers.

I was back inside the house by 9:15 p.m. with a half-full bag of the most boring candy anybody had ever seen. And even worse than that, a police car rode through our neighborhood the whole time we were trick-or-treating. None of us recognized the officer. He didn't bother us—but after the incident with Kari, I got a little shaky when I saw police cars now. Then, when Brent, Jas, and I went our separate ways to go home, I noticed the officer again, parked on my block, watching me.

22

My first year at the Grove hadn't started well. When I think about it, it actually sucked. Both Mya and Kari had left, and the rest of us would probably have to move before the school year was over. I didn't have much to be happy about these days. Halloween was a bust, and I never found the missing piece from my superhero puzzle.

The next afternoon, when the bell rang to dismiss us from social studies, Mr. Baker asked me to stay after class. I couldn't think of anything I'd done wrong. My grade wasn't the best, but I didn't have any late assignments either. I sat quietly while the other kids rushed toward the door.

I waved Brent and Alyssa to go on just in case things went worse than I thought. Then I waited for Mr. Baker to tell me what this was all about.

"Wesley, I read the opening for your report. It was just fine, but I wanted to ask you why you chose climate change as your topic," he said, walking over to my desk.

"I . . . I chose climate change because . . . it's a

big deal right now and . . . ," I started. The truth is, I hadn't figured out how to explain climate change without making it sound super unexciting—Mr. Baker wouldn't let me get away with that.

"Go on," Mr. Baker said, waiting for me to stay something that made sense. When I didn't, he said, "This project isn't only a big part of your grade; it's a way for you to connect to the world around you. That's why I let each of you pick your own topics. If climate change isn't connecting with you—show us what is."

I decided to be honest. It couldn't hurt, and I was running out of time. "I couldn't think of anything that I really wanted to write about, so I kinda got my topic from someone else," I said.

"I think there's something *really* important happening in your community right now," Mr. Baker said with a slight grin. At least it looked like a grin.

"Yeah, but the class won't care about that," I said, more to myself than to him. "And I already don't like talking in front of people. It'll be even worse if they don't care about my topic."

"You can make them care," Mr. Baker said. "And don't get hung up on the presentation—just add some of your personality to it," he added.

I hadn't cared when Kari and the other families were being forced out—but I did care now. Maybe I did need a topic that impacted me. Not that climate change wasn't important, but maybe Mr. Baker was right—I could make the class care about my community.

"Is it too late for me to change my topic?" I asked.

"It's a little late in the game, but if anyone can do it, I know you can."

So I guess I had a new topic . . . gentrification. I needed to get to work. I went straight home to redo my paper. I had to make gentrification interesting enough to write about *and* think of a way not to have a boring presentation. I didn't want to answer to Mr. Baker (or Mom and Dad either) for not giving my best.

I hopped online to see how many other communities were going through the same thing as the Oaks. Maybe that would keep the class's attention. I typed *Where does gentrification happen?* in the search bar. I got 2,610,000 results—this was going to take a while.

I flipped through article after article about families being forced out of cities, only for their original homes to be taken over by younger, more affluent residents. *Affluent* meant rich and white, or at least it seemed that way.

The more I read, the swimmier my thoughts got.

Then I saw an article titled "Stop Gentrification Before It Starts." The article talked about how a small town near the North Carolina coast stopped gentrification in its tracks by getting their neighborhood registered on the National Register of Historic Places. No new construction could happen without approval, which kept their neighborhood safe from condo buildings.

I rubbed my eyes to make sure I'd really read that right. Maybe it wasn't over—this could work for the Oaks!

Until now, everyone (including me) had been so busy looking for a way to stop Simmons, no one had thought about researching Kensington Oaks. Maybe that was the answer.

■ ■ ■

Over the next few days, I visited the library every chance I got. I put my old librarian skills to work and found everything I could about the history of Kensington Oaks. I looked through old newspaper clippings and even watched old TV news reports.

A lot of the stuff I found was useless, like this area being known for its oak trees (duh) or the unbelievably low crime in our neighborhood. This was stuff I already knew—so much for me getting excited about nothing.

But then this afternoon, I found something interesting. In a column written about local entrepreneurs, I read that Kensington Oaks and its surrounding neighborhoods were once called Pippin Village, after a man named Frederick Pippin.

Now, this was something to get excited about. Mr. Pippin was a Black entrepreneur who owned and operated a small lumber mill during the 1930s. It was the only Black-owned lumber mill in the state.

Is this real? I thought. I couldn't read the words fast enough.

Even though Mr. Pippin didn't get much support from the city, he grew his lumber mill on his own and employed over seventy-five workers. To help his employees, he bought the land surrounding the mill and built a community of small homes. He rented those homes to the millworkers so they would be close to work. With a group of hardworking families, Pippin Village started to do well.

Pippin Village caught the attention of local law enforcement and politicians. Seeing Black families be successful on their own made people angry. The city started to harass Mr. Pippin. They fined him for noise and trash violations. They even arrested his workers.

Mr. Pippin fought back as best he could by keeping his community employed, but as he got older, he gave up on fighting the city and decided to close his lumber mill. When the mill closed, the workers moved out of the houses and Mr. Pippin sold them. Over the next sixty years, the old Pippin Village land was bought and sold and bought and sold lots of times.

Just thirty years ago, the area was bought again and Kensington Oaks was born. The original Pippin Village homes had been torn down, but the neighborhood still looked a lot like it did back then.

How could I not have known this? Mr. Pippin was a legend in this city, or least he should be, a legend stripped of his legacy.

I'd cracked a mysterious code. I had no idea what to do next, but I did know who to ask. The only person I knew who'd lived in the Oaks longer than Mom.

I ran the whole way to visit my favorite storyteller.

"Hey, Mr. Hank," I called out when I reached his driveway. He was rolling an old-timey spiked steel thingy across his front yard.

He stopped rolling when he saw me. "Hey, Wes, you come to help me turn this grass over?"

"Ummm . . ." The last thing I wanted to do was yard work.

"I'm teasing you. Sit on down. I need a break anyway."

I headed to the steps of his front porch while Mr. Hank stomped his mud-covered boots in the grass (what was left of it) and plopped down beside me on the bottom step. He pulled his gloves off and tossed them on the ground beside his boots. The smell of soap, sweat, and wet dirt wafted from his body and hung in the air.

"Don't you ever get tired of working on this grass?" I asked.

"I'm just blessed that I have the strength to get out here and do it. Besides, if I don't, who gon' do it? You?" Mr. Hank said, giving me a nudge.

I laughed to myself. I had no plans on turning grass or whatever he called it. I didn't mind cutting the yard, but that was where my landscaping skills stopped.

"Mr. Hank, have you ever heard of a man named Frederick Pippin?"

"I can't say that I have," he said.

"Okay . . . well, do you know how Kensington Oaks got its name?"

"Hmmm, let me guess: Maxine gave you a project, and you trying to skip the work and get me to answer for you."

"No, nothing like that," I said, trying to hold back a grin. "For real, I promise."

"You know what, Wes, I really don't know. I always figured it was named after some rich family, probably related to the British royals."

"Kensington Oaks like Kensington Palace?"

"Maybe so. Oh, and of course all these oak trees."

He shrugged and tipped his head toward the large patch of trees in his backyard.

I wondered if anybody knew who was in charge of naming the Oaks. I hoped it wasn't after the British royal family—I mean, they did have a Black duchess for a while, but they were still way too fancy for the Oaks.

After a few more minutes, Mr. Hank got back to his grass turning and I headed to my side of the street. I couldn't seem to shake the thought of my neighborhood being named after some rich royal people. Even if that wasn't true, it didn't seem fair that nobody knew who Mr. Pippin was—not even Mr. Hank, and he knew everything.

23

I waited until Mom and Dad were comfortable on the couch the next evening after dinner before I snuck into my room with the phone.

"Save Our City, this is Monica speaking," a sweet voice poured into my ear.

"Ms. Monica?" I hadn't expected anyone to answer this late. I'd pumped myself up to leave a message, not have a real conversation.

"Yes, Wesley? Is this Wesley?"

"Yes. This is Wes. I mean, Wesley. I was calling because you told me to get creative, and I think I have a good idea to stop Simmons Development Group."

"Okay, I'm listening," Ms. Monica said.

"Can we meet tomorrow, after school in Mr. Baker's class? I have a lot to show you."

"Of course. See you then."

That night in bed, images of kings and queens filled my head. Kensington Oaks was the most regular-degular neighborhood around; there was no way we were named after some fancy people dressed in velvet short pants, long socks, and pointy shoes.

Ms. Monica was right on time for our meeting the next day. I'd also invited Mr. Baker—I figured he could help too. I was so hyped that before they could sit down, I started explaining everything I'd found about Mr. Pippin and Pippin Village and what I'd read about that other town and the historic designation.

I rambled on and on about the mill, and how the city officials ran Mr. Pippin off, and how the Oaks should be named after him, not some royal people.

Mr. Baker turned to Ms. Monica and asked, "Did you know any of this?"

"I'm ashamed to say I didn't," she said.

"Me either," Mr. Baker said.

"He was the first Black mill owner in the state," I added. I knew that had to be a big deal—back then Black people didn't hardly own anything.

"Unfortunately, this happens a lot to Black people's history," Mr. Baker said. "Their achievements are often buried or stolen."

Dad had told me stories of that happening a lot with musicians and inventors back in the day.

"I think the city hated him so much that they just acted like he was never here," I said. It kinda made me sad to think about all the good he'd done creating jobs and a whole community, and no one even knew about it.

Mr. Baker was super quiet. I didn't even hear him breathing. Maybe I was talking too much.

Then Mr. Baker took a deep breath and said, "Wesley, I'm so proud of you for finding this. Even if the state doesn't designate Kensington Oaks a historic district, you've discovered a historic hero in Frederick Pippin."

I was proud of me too. This could really help the Oaks and show people how important Frederick Pippin was.

"I've never gotten a district designated as historic—it takes a lot of paperwork and time and a lot of luck. But I'm certainly up for the challenge, and you have the full support of Save Our City!" Ms. Monica said.

"For real?" I asked.

"Yes, you do. Give me what you have so far and we'll figure out what's needed to file the paperwork."

"Okay, sure. . . . It's just, I do have one problem . . . ," I started, lowering my voice. "My parents kinda banned me from working on the Simmons offer."

"Kinda banned?" Mr. Baker asked.

"Well, banned . . . like a complete ban," I said.

"What happened?" Ms. Monica asked. "I thought they were okay with you helping."

"Well . . . I haven't exactly been keeping up with my schoolwork . . . ," I said.

"This process stops right here until you get your parents on board," Mr. Baker said.

"Yes sir."

"After you get your parents' permission, I'll be happy to help," Ms. Monica said.

I nodded. "One more thing, Mr. Baker. I was wondering if I could have more time on my fall project. Maybe a couple of weeks? I want to add the information about Mr. Pippin to my presentation, but I don't think it will be ready in time," I said.

"I'll give you an extension on your presentation, but your report has to be turned in on Monday," Mr. Baker said.

I headed home with a twisted-up feeling. Mom and Dad had said the adults needed to handle this, and I'd gone behind their backs. I knew they'd be happy to learn about Mr. Pippin; I just needed them to tag me back in so I could help.

■ ■ ■

The next morning, I paced my bedroom floor back and forth, trying to think of the best way to tell my parents that I'd disobeyed an order. The clock on my nightstand blinked 00:00—it was old and needed new batteries—but I guessed it was around seven-thirty. I decided to just present the facts. They would understand why I did it. *Right?* I hoped so.

It was Saturday; the music should be starting any moment. I stopped pacing and sat on the end of my bed, waiting for the first sound of life outside of my room. As soon as Mary J. Blige's raspy voice filled the air, I knew it was time. I crept down the hallway to the kitchen and found Mom half sweeping the kitchen floor, half dancing while Dad danced behind her.

"Excuse me," I said loudly, before they could get any closer.

"Good morning, sweetie," Mom said.

At least she's in a good mood.

I took a deep breath. "So . . . I found something interesting when I was working on my social studies project. Can I show it to you?"

"Sure, we'll look at it later," Dad said, his face buried in Mom's neck.

"It's kinda important," I said. "Can I show it to you now?"

"Of course you can," Mom said, easing away from Dad.

"Okay, good!" I said.

They grabbed a seat on the couch while I ran to my room to get the research I'd collected. I came back and placed the overflowing folder of articles, pictures, and newspaper clippings on the table in front of them and explained that I'd switched my topic from climate change to gentrification.

"About eighty-five years ago, Kensington Oaks was called Pippin Village," I started. "It was named after Frederick Pippin, a Black man who owned a lumber mill and a bunch of houses on this land."

I went on to tell them everything I'd learned and how the history of Mr. Pippin had been buried. I kept expecting them to yell at me for not dropping it when they told me to, but right in the middle of my explanation Mom pulled me over and gave me a hug. I took in the smell of lemony floor cleaner on her skin and let her hold me for a minute.

"Son, this is incredible. You found all of this? On your own?" Dad asked.

"Well . . . yeah . . . I was looking for something to add to my presentation, but when I saw how another community dealt with gentrification, I was thinking we could use this information to get the Oaks named historic, and then Simmons can't redevelop it."

"That sounds great, but I'm pretty sure that process is a long, hard road," Dad said.

"It's better than waiting for Simmons to kick us out and build another condo building," I said. "We have to protect our history, right?"

Dad smiled. He knew that I'd just used his line against him.

"Wes is right," Mom said to Dad.

Mom was on my side. I wanted to jump up and down, but I decided against it. The last time I got this excited—when the first offer expired—that good feeling was over quick.

"So, can we try to get the designation?" I asked, looking at Dad.

"Let's see what we need to do," he said.

From what I read about getting a community named a historic place, Kensington Oaks had to have some kind of important historical buildings, structures, or objects and proof of their importance. Mom, Dad, and I went back through all the pictures and articles looking for something we could use. And after an hour, we'd come up empty.

When we didn't find anything after another hour, Mom got on the phone to talk to Ms. Monica about what we needed to file the paperwork with the National Register of Historic Places through our State Historic Preservation Office. We also decided to keep this new strategy and the information about Pippin Village just between us for now. We couldn't risk word of it getting out to Simmons Development Group. I couldn't wait to spring it on them like, *bam!*

24

Monday morning during homeroom, I caught myself staring over at Mya's old desk. The class had voted to retire it like an old NBA jersey, so there it sat—empty. Only Mya could get a desk retired after only a month and a half. Alyssa said she was doing fine at her new school and even asked about me on Halloween, but I wasn't ready to talk to her yet.

"Hi, Wes." Alyssa interrupted me from my thoughts. The smell of cocoa butter and vanilla lingered around her. I couldn't tell if it was her hair or skin—it could have been both. Her braided-up ponytail was tied with a green ribbon. It matched her dress perfectly.

"I didn't see your name on the presentation list for today. When do you go?" she asked.

"Ummm, I finished my report, but I'm not ready to do my presentation yet. Mr. Baker said I could have a little more time."

I hated keeping anything from her, but I couldn't talk about my new research yet. We weren't sure the historic designation would work, and with her mom being on the board, we couldn't risk word getting out.

For the first time all year, I was excited for social studies block. Both Alyssa and Brent were presenting, and I couldn't wait to see their presentations.

Brent went first.

He was cool as iced tea when he approached the front of the class—something I only wished I could be. His topic was "Preserving the First Amendment." He started by explaining that the First Amendment gives us the freedom to practice whatever religion we choose, freedom of the press to report things, freedoms of assembly and petition, and freedom of speech to not get into trouble for saying what we think. Brent's focus was on how the freedom of speech of athletes was being violated and slowly taken away because some people think athletes should just play sports and not talk about things going on in the world around us.

It was the least boring social studies presentation I'd ever seen—Brent even had the *SportsCenter* theme music playing during his intro.

He also included a slideshow that displayed over twenty instances of football, basketball, soccer, and baseball players being punished for speaking out against social injustices, like police brutality.

His closing line was a quote by Colin Kaepernick: *"I'm going to speak the truth when I'm asked about it. This isn't for look. This isn't for publicity or anything like that.*

This is for people that don't have the voice." That last line made me think about Kari and how Officer Stewart had silenced his voice. At the end of his presentation, Brent dropped to one knee in front of the class to drive home the point. Of course, he got a standing ovation.

After Brent's presentation, Jaslene did hers on immigration rights and Dex did his on climate change—it was really good, so I'm glad I didn't do mine on the same thing.

Alyssa's was the last presentation of the day. I knew she'd kill it. She'd chosen women's rights as her topic. Her voice was calm and confident as she explained how even at our ages we should be thinking about preserving women's rights.

The boys in class shifted nervously in their seats, trying to avoid Alyssa's eyes.

This was nothing new to me; Mom had preached this sermon before. Just this spring, I'd marched in a women's rights rally. Dad and I were the only men there yelling, "My body, my rules!"

Alyssa passed around photographs of women and girls marching together in rallies all over the country. She told us about the pay gap between men and women and especially between men and Black women. Black women earn only sixty-one cents for every dollar white men earn. Then she explained how Black women aren't treated the same as white women, mainly with medical treatment in the United States, because doctors don't always believe them.

My favorite part of her presentation was a video-taped interview with her mom. Ms. Watkins talked about her own experience with childbirth. When she was pregnant with Alyssa, she was rushed to the hospital twice—both times she was sent back home. At some point, she got really sick and had to have an emergency birth.

Alyssa was born two months early and stayed in the hospital for a whole month. Her mom almost died during the delivery. Ms. Watkins ended her interview by saying, "I believe I got worse care because I am a Black woman."

Alyssa finished with "Black women are almost four times as likely as white women to die from pregnancy- or childbirth-related causes."

After the video was over, the whole class sat silent, our butts glued to our seats. The air was smog thick. Mr. Baker let us sit there quietly until the bell rang. I was so proud of Alyssa. I knew how hard it must have been to share that much of herself with the class.

"Alyssa," I said, walking over to her. "You did a great job."

"Thanks. I wasn't sure about showing the video, but I'm glad I did."

"You know, my mom had some bad stuff happen when I was born too. That's the reason I'm an only child."

"I thought you always said there was only room in the family for one fresh Henderson." Alyssa smiled a smile sweet enough to warm up my insides. I felt even closer to her now. We were cut from the same cloth, like Mr. Hank would say.

25

Brent was leaving.

Dad told me, not Brent. Without warning, my legs got noodley. I would've collapsed on the floor if the couch hadn't caught me.

My friendship with Brent was in this strange back-and-forth game—like an endless Ping-Pong match with no winner. We weren't fighting or anything, and he was still my best friend, even if neither of us was acting like it.

Deep down I'd known it was possible he would leave, but I never thought it would really happen. Simmons had been hard at work trying to get families to accept the new offer. Mom and Dad had gotten three more calls from them just last week. I figured someone would give in, but I hated that Brent and his parents were the first family to take the offer.

After I heard, I called him to ask about it.

"My dad told me y'all are moving . . . ," I said.

"Yeah, it's true," Brent answered.

"Dang, that's messed up."

"Yeah . . ."

I sighed. "So, when you leaving?"

"Not sure, but soon. . . . We already found another house."

"Oh . . . dang. Where is it?"

"Like fifteen minutes away."

"You still going to the Grove?"

"Yeah, of course."

I sighed again but felt a little better. "Well, see you around, then."

"Yeah, see you around," said Brent.

That left me with nothing else to say. It was really happening.

On the day of the move, I watched from my bedroom window as Brent's dad, Mr. Williams, backed the moving truck into their driveway. Their house was on the street behind mine. There was nothing but a raggedy fence and an overgrown oak tree separating our backyards. I remembered six years ago when I'd watched the Williamses move in.

It was a muggy summer day and we'd just finished dinner. I watched from the kitchen window, excited to have a new kid move in, and he looked like he was my age. He'd kicked his football over the fence and was attempting to climb over after it. A lady appeared at his back door and yelled for him to get down. She said he could get the ball in the morning.

I'd waited and waited the next morning for him to

come. While I ate breakfast, I'd watched for the boy to appear and try to climb the fence again. When he didn't, me and Dad went over to take it ourselves. I begged Dad for a whole hour before he said yes. I tucked the football under my arm and knocked on the door. It swung open and there was a tall, dark-skinned boy with a grin as wide as his face. "I'm Brent," he said. I knew right away we would be best friends.

Brent and I spent the next six years doing everything together—playing video games, shooting hoops, cracking jokes—everything. Our parents said we were brothers, and even though I knew we weren't, I wished we were.

Maybe that's why it felt like somebody was kickboxing my heart as I watched Brent pack his stuff into the moving truck. I knew I would have to go over and say goodbye, but I didn't want to.

I pulled my hoodie low and tight and headed toward the fence. I hopped it with one easy jump. Brent was waiting for me with the same smile he always wore. "What took you so long?" he asked.

I put on a phony smile and said, "I was waiting for you to do all the heavy lifting." Brent punched my arm and laughed. We stood there tossing random chatter back and forth. Then Brent brought up how big their new house was.

"It has a whole extra room. My mom said we could use it for when people sleep over," he said.

"Oh yeah? That's cool," I said, more to myself than to him.

We went on trading words I would never remember. The lump in my throat got bigger every time I saw another box lifted into the truck.

When all the boxes were loaded, Mr. Williams called Brent inside for one last sweep. I followed Brent into his room. A gloomy haze hovered over us. This was it, the last time I would be in Brent's room. No more wrestling on his too-little bed. No more banging out beats on the door of his closet—it had the perfect bass. No more fake study sessions while we snuck to play NBA 2K instead.

I thought about who would move in next. No matter who it was, they would never replace my best friend. Brent must have read my mind, because he said, "I bet some corny kid will move in after we're gone." I wasn't in a laughing mood, but I giggled a little just to make Brent feel good.

We made our way to the front of the house and out the door. Brent's parents were waiting.

"Now, Wes, you are always welcome to come over. You know that. After we get settled in, you can come stay the night," Mrs. Williams said. It was a nice thing to say, but I knew it wouldn't be the same—things were changing, like Mya had said. Brent was another piece of my puzzle breaking away.

He dapped me up and got in the truck. Before they could pull out of the driveway, I had hopped back across the fence. I didn't want to watch the truck drive away.

26

Stacks of old articles and faded black-and-white photographs covered our kitchen table Saturday morning. Mom, Dad, Mr. Baker, Ms. Monica, and I had spent the morning huddled up, poring over every bit of information we could find on Pippin Village. My eyes had gotten heavy from staring at my research and looking for something to connect then to now—something with historical significance. I knew Mr. Pippin was the man in his day, but we still hadn't found what we needed for the designation.

Ms. Monica explained that the designation wouldn't bring our neighbors back, but it would likely stop any large buildings, like a condo building, from going up in the Oaks. That meant Simmons wouldn't be so interested in our neighborhood because they couldn't build a big, fancy place like they'd planned—and that was enough for me.

"We'll need some kind of symbol that ties back to Pippin Village," Ms. Monica said. "Let's keep looking."

I gazed at the photographs. The lumber mill took up the space where the corner store used to be and where the library is now, and the village spanned ten blocks east of it, pretty close to where the houses are now. The village homes were identical in size and shape, with little porches on the front. There were two main pathways on each side of the community connecting the village to the mill. I imagined the kids standing on their porches waving to their fathers as they walked to work.

Photos of the inside of Pippin's Lumber Mill showed men standing side by side working together. In one photo, the workers posed under the sign at the entrance of the mill. Their faces showed no expression at all, but they had happy eyes. Boys as young as me stood proudly beside their fathers. I wondered if they worked there too. My favorite picture was of Mr. Pippin. He stood under the lumber mill sign beside his employees, with a strong, wide stance.

Even after looking for hours, we still hadn't found what we needed. Ms. Monica had said this would be hard, but right now it seemed impossible.

■ ■ ■

The next morning I got up early to meet Jas and Alyssa at the basketball court. There was no sign of Drip or any of the older guys, so we had the whole court to ourselves. We played a game of HORSE and talked about how weird it was with Brent gone.

"This is the first time he won't be around for Thanksgiving," Jas said. "He always had me save him some quindim—it's his favorite dessert."

"And he always begged my mom for pecan pie," Alyssa said.

Brent has a thing for desserts, and we knew to save him something sweet from our Thanksgiving meals. I guess we didn't have to anymore.

"I think Kari is coming over for Thanksgiving," I said, changing the subject. "He might even get to stay the night."

"Let me know if y'all are up for an NBA 2K tournament," Alyssa said, smirking.

"Ummm, yeah . . . we'll let you know," I said. No way was Alyssa beating me again in front of everyone.

We finished our game of HORSE and headed our separate ways. I wondered how many times I'd strolled the 102 steps from my house to the court and how many games of HORSE I'd played during my time in the Oaks. I didn't want to think about not having the park right down the block from me—it was a part of me.

I got washed up, went straight to the kitchen, and spread the pictures from the folder back onto the table.

I held each picture in my hands. I focused on the outside view and then concentrated on the inner details.

When I got to the photo from the day before, the one with the mill workers under the Pippin's Lumber Mill sign, far in the background of the photo a little girl caught my attention. She stood left of the main building by herself. I wondered what she would've been doing at the mill.

Then I saw it!

She was standing in front of a water fountain—it was just a bit shorter than her and had a steel water basin.

Could it have the same swirly leaves around the base as the fountain in the park?

"Mom, Dad," I yelled. "Come look!"

They came running from their bedroom.

"Wes, what is it?" Dad asked.

"Is this the same fountain that's in the park?" I asked, pointing to the photo. I could barely keep the picture still in my hand.

"I think it is. . . . Could it really be?" Mom asked. She grabbed the photo from me.

They took turns looking at the water fountain through a magnifying glass.

That has to be it.

That must be why I've always felt a connection to

the water fountain. It's the final missing piece of the Pippin puzzle.

I imagined the children from Pippin Village playing on the very land I've lived on my whole life—standing on the same ground where I play basketball, even drinking from the same water fountain.

"Wes, I think you're right. This could be the same fountain," Dad said.

"That should be enough to get us on the registry, right?" I asked.

"Let's call Monica," Dad said.

I waited while Dad explained how the fountain looked exactly like the one in the neighborhood park. Then he put the phone on speaker. "There are no guarantees, but I think we have a very convincing argument," Ms. Monica said. "I'll submit the application, and in forty-five days we'll know if we are approved."

■ ■ ■

The next few days crept by on the back of a caterpillar. I'd poured all my energy into books and research for weeks, and now there was nothing left to do except wait. "Good things come to those who wait," Mr. Hank always says.

Forty-two days days left of waiting.

I laid the pieces of my puzzle out on the kitchen table. I had completed it at least a dozen times. It was one of my favorites. "Eyes in the Wild" was a close-up of a lion in its natural habitat. Something about the big, golden mane and powerful posture drew me in.

If no one bothered me, I could complete this five-hundred-piece puzzle in two hours flat. I'd been so antsy lately; fixing puzzles was like a breath of fresh air.

"Want some company?" Mom asked, joining me in the kitchen.

"Ummm, okay," I said. I would rather have been left alone, but I couldn't think of a way to say no. Besides, it was her house and her table and she had no problem reminding me of that.

"Need some help?"

"Nah, I'm trying for a new record."

I turned the pieces faceup and got busy with the outside border.

"I'll just watch, then." She settled into the chair across from me with a cup of tea and watched me work.

Mom cleared her throat. The easy, cool air started to warm. Mom cleared her throat again. The air got warmer. Mom cleared her throat again. I knew she wanted to say something—when she had something on her mind, she randomly cleared her throat over and over. I waited. The speech was coming.

"You know, Wes," she started, "not everyone is gifted

with the fight and drive you have. That thing deep inside pushing you to seek out your own way, that's called being a leader."

I kept my eyes fixed on the puzzle. I painstakingly fit the pieces together one by one. *So much for setting a new record.*

"That's not something to take lightly. You have it. You're a natural-born leader," she said.

I wasn't so sure I was a leader, natural or unnatural.

Mom sat quietly watching me a bit longer. Then she drank the last of her tea and got up from the table.

"Don't stay up too late," she said after planting a light kiss on my forehead.

I give Mom a hard time, but I knew she was trying to help. The thing is, Mom is a leader—at everything, really. When she walks into a room, she controls it. She always says the right words, and I've never seen her back down from a challenge.

She does it all: PTA meetings, class volunteer, chaperone, awesome cook, and a decent basketball player. I would never admit it to her, but my mom is pretty dope.

I'm not sure I'll ever be the leader she is.

I fit the last puzzle piece in place. Something about how each part fit so perfect and exact made me envious.

27

Every fall, I love going to the pre-Thanksgiving football game at the local high school. Dad went to school at East Wood High and makes a point to go back every year for this game. I was looking forward to it more than ever this year; I needed something fun to distract me from worrying about getting approved for the historic designation. Dad and I, dressed in matching silver-and-blue hoodies, jumped into the SUV, ready to cheer on the Wildcats.

During the short five-mile drive to the high school, we were transported to another place—a place way nicer than what I remembered. The neighborhoods around East Wood High used to be made up of small, old homes. Now in their place were rows of three-story stone-front town houses. The apartment buildings that once backed up to the school had been torn down and replaced with a block of partially built mini-mansions. I'm talking houses that looked like they'd probably be two or three times the size of mine when they were finished.

"Dad, when did all this happen?" I asked.

"Not sure, Wes. I knew there had been some improvements—you remember the construction from last year—but I had no idea the whole neighborhood had been overhauled," Dad replied. I could tell he was just as confused as I was. His eyebrows were stuck in an up position, like he'd just seen a ghost.

The park across the street from the school was now just an open, bland slab of concrete. In the middle of the slab was a grid of holes spraying water in different directions—a fountain for rich people. Little wooden tables and chairs, painted a vivid green, were placed just outside the reach of the water holes. Not one swing in sight. It looked more like an outdoor dining room than a park.

Dad drove around to the entrance of the school. The old parking lot was blocked off with bright orange construction cones. There was an attendant directing cars to the rear of the building. When we reached the new lot at the back of the school, I realized the old East Wood High was practically gone. Everything from the walkways to the paint was new.

We climbed the stairs to enter the football stadium. The original stadium had been updated with new seats, a turf field, and huge high-definition monitors. The normally Black crowd was sprinkled with more white people than I could count, cheering on the team.

Dad and I marched down and grabbed seats near the fifty-yard line.

Before our butts could hit the seats, a deep voice called out, "Hey, Walt!"

A man who looked about Dad's age waved from a spot a couple seats away. He was decked out in Wildcats gear from head to toe. He wore a full sweat suit, a hat, and a flag draped over his shoulders—I would have never let Dad leave the house like that.

"Come on over, I've got two empty seats," the man said.

"Big Reg? Hey. How are you?" Dad said as he and I walked over to the open seats. "You remember Mr. Reggie, right?" Dad asked, turning to me. "We went to East Wood together."

I nodded, but I didn't remember him at all.

Mr. Reggie gave Dad a hard pat on the back and reached out a firm hand to me. Mr. Reggie was indeed big, like security guard big. His hand swallowed mine.

"My son's a wide receiver on the team. He was MVP last year. I'm glad you'll get to see him play," Mr. Reggie said as the first snap signaled the start of the game.

I've never been a huge football fan—basketball is more my game—but I like visiting Dad's old school. I'll eventually be going to high school at East Wood.

Dad thinks it's cool that I'll be walking the same halls he did.

"Go, go, go! Touchdown!" Mr. Reggie yelled.

The crowd erupted, and the cheerleaders ran up the sideline cheering the team on.

"Black players, white cheerleaders. Boy, I tell you, this isn't the same old East Wood," Mr. Reggie said with a teeth smack.

"All this happened fast," Dad said, lowering his voice. "I didn't even recognize the neighborhood. Last year they had just started breaking ground on the lot across the street."

"It did happen fast. Those homes went up, and everything else followed," Mr. Reggie explained, pointing toward the town houses. "What bothers me is all these improvements to the school happened when the rich white people moved in. That old parking lot has been in bad shape for years. Same for the inside of the school. It wasn't until we moved out and they moved in that someone spent some money to update the place."

"We're afraid the same thing will happen in our neighborhood," Dad said. His voice sounded small, maybe even a little scared.

"Well, I can tell you, we took the money and ran. We moved four miles down the hill," Mr. Reggie said. "We figured they won't cross the tracks, with all these shiny new houses." Mr. Reggie had a deep growl in his voice, but his eyes looked as sad as Dad's did.

I listened quietly and thought about Mr. Baker's article, "Is Gentrification the New Segregation?" I wasn't sure, but it was starting to seem that way, considering Mr. Reggie had moved out of his neighborhood and now it was filling up with white people. The same way the Oaks was once all white and when Mom moved in it slowly turned mostly Black. The same thing was happening around East Wood, but in reverse. Yeah, maybe segregation was back.

28

A few days later, I woke up to the smell of cinnamon and nutmeg floating through the air. I knew that meant the kitchen counter was lined with Mom's famous sweet potato pies. She always makes one special pie that's all for me. A perk of being an only child.

Since it was Thanksgiving Day, I'd have to announce what I was most thankful for before dinner was served. This year was especially tough because nothing was the same. My world had been dumped on its head—like a turtle stuck on its back, waving its arms and legs, trying to get right side up again.

I could say I was thankful for new sneakers, but that would earn me a slap on the back of the head. Maybe I could say I was thankful to have somewhere to live, but that would be a lie. Besides, I wasn't sure the Oaks would be my home much longer. I *was* thankful Kari was coming to Thanksgiving dinner. It had been over a month since he moved away, and even though we talked on the phone sometimes, it wasn't the same.

Mom was busy in the kitchen. Every pot and pan was out on the counters. She always prepares the whole meal by herself; she says it's her gift to her favorite men (me and Dad).

"Hey, Mom, smells good. Need some help?" I asked when I joined her in the kitchen.

"No, I got it. You just hang out and rest up—it's your night to do the dishes," she said with a wink.

"What time will Kari get here?"

"Soon. Tasha asked if we could do dinner a little early this year so she could get back home. She also said it'll be fine for Kari to stay for a couple days."

"Yes! Thanks, Mom."

I got busy thinking of all the stuff me and Kari could do over the weekend. Maybe Jas and Brent could come over too and we could watch movies.

■ ■ ■

Ding dong!

"That's Kari! I'll get it!" I said, opening the front door.

"Happy Thanksgiving, everyone," Ms. Tasha said as she and Kari came inside.

"Hey," Kari said softly.

"Where's Danica?" I asked.

"She stayed back with her aunt to help with the big family dinner. I promised I'd be back in time to eat with them, but I know how much Kari wanted to be here for the traditional Hendersons' Thanksgiving meal," Ms. Tasha said.

After Kari's dad left, he, Danica, and Ms. Tasha started coming to our house for Thanksgiving dinner, since Ms. Tasha usually worked right up to dinnertime. Mom said it gave them one less thing to worry about on a day that should be about thankfulness.

"Come on in and get comfortable," Mom called from the kitchen. "Dinner's almost ready."

Dad was parked in his favorite spot on the couch, his eyes glued to the play-by-play action of the football game. I sat with him and made a spot for Kari between us. Instead, Kari slumped down on the far end with his back to the TV.

I didn't know what was up with him. I knew he wasn't into sports, but he usually pretended a little better than this.

Ding dong!

"Hey, Wes. Happy Thanksgiving, y'all!" Mr. Hank said when I opened the door.

Mr. Hank was always right on time for dinner. Dad flicked off the TV and joined Mom in the kitchen.

"Gather round, everyone. Grab the nearest hand— let's bless this food and dig in," Dad said, holding Mom's hand. Everyone squeezed up to the round table meant for four people. I was sandwiched between Kari and Mr. Hank. It wasn't until I reached for Kari's hand that

I noticed his purple, bruised knuckles. He snatched his hand away and tucked it into his pocket.

"Dear Lord, thank you for this wonderful meal prepared by my lovely wife," Dad said. "Thank you for another opportunity to break bread with family and friends."

I peeked over at Kari. He sat motionless. His eyes were wide open, but even the white part looked dark.

"Amen," everyone said at once, everyone except Kari.

I think Mom could tell Kari wasn't feeling very thankful. So instead of making us go around the table to say what we were thankful for, she just said, "I am thankful for my family and my home and happy we have created such a special tradition with everyone at this table. Now, let's eat."

The dinner conversation was mostly Mr. Hank telling stories about his days in the army, only to be interrupted by an occasional joke by Dad. That's the way Thanksgiving has been for years. Mr. Hank commanded the room, and I loved every moment of it. The more Mr. Hank talked, the less I had to.

It wasn't until someone else noticed Kari's injured hand that things turned bad.

"Kari, what happened to your hand?" Mom asked.

"Huh? Nothing. It's no big deal, Mrs. Maxine."

"No big deal, huh? You may as well tell 'em," Ms. Tasha interjected.

Kari sat silent with his hands folded in his lap.

"He got in a fight. Apparently, they been pickin' on him at that new school. Principal said Kari should have walked away. 'Cause he didn't, they suspended him for two weeks," Ms. Tasha said.

"Kari, how long has this been going on? Wasn't there someone you could tell?" Mom asked.

Kari said nothing.

The temperature in the room started to rise as everyone stared in Kari's direction. I wanted to jump in and say something, but I knew better than to get in grown folks' conversation.

"Say something, Kari." Ms. Tasha glared at him.

"Ain't nothing to say," Kari finally spat out.

And that was that.

Thankfully, Mr. Hank started another story. He told everyone about the time he and his squad got into a brawl at a bar in Bangkok. "I escaped with just a black eye, but the other guys . . . hmmm, let's just say I'm here to talk about it."

That cooled things down a bit, but I couldn't wait to talk to Kari and find out what had really happened.

After dinner, us boys were sent to the kitchen to bust the suds, my least favorite thing to do, but I would have some alone time with Kari. We stood there quiet while the sink filled up with hot, soapy water. Kari was like an ice statue. Cold and hard.

"You gonna tell me the real story?" I asked.

"Like I said, ain't nothing to tell," Kari said in a flat tone.

"Something happened. Look at your hand."

"I got in a fight. Some kid was picking at my clothes, all right?"

"All right." I decided to leave it alone.

The rest of the dishwashing session went along with not much talking at all. Except for the chatter in my head. *When is Ms. Tasha gonna get Kari some new clothes? Of course kids will pick at him if he wears the same stuff over and over.*

When the suds were bust, we went back into the living room. Mr. Hank was in the middle of another Bangkok story.

"Mom, can we leave?" Kari blurted out of nowhere.

"Kari, stop it. The Hendersons made this great meal for us," Ms. Tasha said.

"Aren't you staying for the weekend?" I asked Kari. I tried to hide the sting from Kari wanting to leave.

"What's the point? I may as well just leave now," he answered.

"Wait a minute, Kari, let's talk—" Dad said.

"Talk for what? No one cares about what I have to

say," Kari interrupted. Then he turned to Dad. "And I have my own family, remember?" He stormed past Ms. Tasha and out the front door.

Cold and hard.

"I'm sorry, y'all, I can't get him to act right. I think it's best we go on home," Ms. Tasha said.

And just like that, Thanksgiving was over and Kari was gone. Again.

29

A Place Called Home had a special day-after-Thanksgiving dinner—and of course I had to serve. I'd thought about asking Jas and Alyssa to come along, but I knew they wouldn't want to spend their Thanksgiving break at the shelter. Maybe they would've said yes, but I'd decided to handle this one with just me and Dad while Mom rested after cooking dinner for everyone the day before.

On the ride over to the shelter, Dad kept trying to bring up Kari storming out, but I didn't want to talk about it. I wanted to get this dinner over with and go back home.

We arrived just as the line started to form outside. We slipped inside the back door, out of the cold air, and into the kitchen to help get things ready.

"Wassup, Wes?" Brent called out from the other side of the kitchen.

"Brent? What are you doing here?"

It had been almost two weeks since he left the Oaks. He'd moved to a neighborhood past East Wood High. He still went to school at the Grove, but the walks to and from school weren't the same without him.

"I could lie and say I wanted to help serve . . . but my dad made me come."

I laughed—Brent always kept it one hundred.

Ms. Grave put me and Brent in charge of the drink station. We filled plastic cups with sweet tea, unsweet tea, or lemonade, while Dad set out the tables and chairs.

"Who would want *un*sweet tea?" Brent asked.

"Right? That's what I was thinking!" I said.

Serving today might not be so bad after all—even if it was during Thanksgiving break, having Brent around the neighborhood made things feel a little more normal.

I wished I could've told him before he moved about the chance of having the Oaks made a historic district. Maybe that would have encouraged him and his parents to stay. But I was sworn to secrecy. Ms. Monica said that because no one knew about Frederick Pippin and Pippin Village, we had a higher chance of getting registered. If Simmons found out what we were working on, they might try to do something stupid like steal the fountain—okay, I added that part, but they could do something to block the designation.

When the doors of the shelter opened, the room flooded with people and food. It was Thanksgiving dinner on steroids. There were eight turkeys, six hams, collard greens, potato salad, mac and cheese, sweet potatoes, corn bread, and corn bread dressing—and a whole table of nothing but pies and cakes.

While everyone ate, Brent and I worked side by side. We filled and refilled drinks, collected trash, and did whatever else Ms. Grave asked for help with.

"I appreciate you young men spending your holiday break spreading some love in the community," Ms. Grave said when she passed us on her way to the kitchen with a handful of dirty dishes.

"See, Wes, I'm still as much a part of this community as you are," Brent teased.

I knew he was kidding, but it rubbed me rough. It didn't seem hard at all for Brent to leave the Oaks. "Not really," I said under my breath. "You left me and moved to a bigger house—remember?"

"Dang, chill! I was joking," Brent said. "And I didn't leave *you*. It's not all about you, Wes. You always think it's about you. Plus, we don't have money, like y'all do!"

"Like *we* do?" I said, stepping back from Brent. "This is about more than money!"

"Yeah right! You the one with all the fresh shoes and clothes. Now my parents will have enough money to buy me stuff."

Brent never got new things, and not like I was trying to be all flashy, but I did get new stuff a lot more than he did—not Mya-level new stuff, but more than most of the other kids around here.

"Look, I'm not tryin' to fight," I said. "All I'm saying is our home is more important than a little money."

"I wouldn't call a hundred thousand dollars a little money," Brent said.

I didn't know what to say; that *was* a lot of money. I looked at Brent—the same Brent who had always been on my side—and remembered the only other time we fought, in third grade when he didn't pick me first to be on his team. I'd made a big deal about it, but it turned out Brent was just trying to be nice to a new kid in our class and picked him first instead. I was being kinda selfish then, and maybe I was being selfish now. I was making this about me.

We must have gotten too loud, because Dad shot us a glare from across the room. His eyes said, "I better not have to come over there."

"My bad, Brent," I said, my voice calmer. "I just didn't expect you to really leave. I wish things were the way they used to be."

"Me too," said Brent. "My dad said this was the only way for us to come up, so he took the money."

I did want Brent and his family to have nice things too.

"That makes sense, I guess."

"We good?" Brent asked, reaching his fist over to me.

"We good," I said, returning the pound. It really did feel good to be cool with my best friend again.

■ ■ ■

Jas and I entered the lunch line in the café just ahead of Alyssa and Brent. Alyssa had dumped those boring turkey sandwiches after Mya left the Grove, and now she mostly ate food from the lunch line like us.

"Oh, look, today is create-your-own-chef-salad day. Mya would love this!" Alyssa said, pointing to the chalkboard at the entrance of the lunch line. Someone had drawn little pieces of lettuce and tomato in green and pink chalk.

Alyssa was right; Mya was the only sixth grader I knew who loved salad. She always packed her own lunch, but she would have jumped at the chance to make her own salad. The thought of Mya actually enjoying something at school lunch made me laugh to myself.

"How's Mya, anyway?" Jas asked.

"She's good. She likes her new school, but I think she misses us. She even asked about Kari the other day," Alyssa said, sneaking a quick look at me. "Her family's

Christmas party is in a couple weeks. She wanted me to make sure you guys are coming."

I was kinda glad Mya wanted me to come. After not getting an invitation on Halloween, I wasn't sure if we'd ever talk again.

"I'll be there," Brent said.

"I'm there! I'll never pass up a chance to visit Mya's luxurious house," Jas said, sticking his pinky up like rich people do in the movies.

"Wes?" Alyssa asked.

"You sure she wants me there?" I asked, trying to be cool.

"I'm positive," Alyssa answered.

"Come on, Wes! It won't be any fun if you aren't there," Jas pleaded.

"Okay . . . I guess I'm in," I said. Not that I had much of a choice; my parents got the invitation in the mail last week. We all went to the Coopers' Christmas party every year. And I did kinda miss Mya.

"Perfect!" Alyssa said. "The dress code is formal, so put on your best outfits."

I already knew any party at Mya's house would be fancy, which meant I'd get to see Alyssa all dressed up. I had to be fly. At least I'd finally get to wear my new vest—I'd been waiting for the right time to wear it.

30

Erykah Badu's voice drifted into my room, lulling me back to sleep. For the first time in months, I was able to sleep in on Saturday morning. Between long blinks, I tried to ignore the screeching tires outside my window. I knew what was happening without even rising from my covers.

It was another moving day.

Our neighbors Mr. and Mrs. York had accepted the latest offer from Simmons. Word on the block was, over twenty families had accepted the offer so far. I knew Ms. Monica said change can take a long time, but after all this waiting to hear back about the historic designation, there wouldn't be any Kensington Oaks left to save.

"I can't believe they're leaving. Beverly used to be one of us." Mom's voice echoed. She gave the exact same speech about everyone when she heard they were moving away from Kensington Oaks. I'd heard enough. I brushed my teeth, slipped on a hoodie, and crept out the back door, undetected. I walked around to the front yard and across the street.

"Wassup, Mr. Hank?"

"Nothing but the rent," Mr. Hank replied, leaning forward in his old porch rocker.

Mr. Hank can always make me laugh. Even his corny jokes make me chuckle. I plopped down on the bottom step in front of his house.

"How many trucks today?"

"Two this morning, one last night. The Halls, the Smiths, and Bill. Kinda sad seeing it all end like this," Mr. Hank said with a cloudy look in his eyes.

"Can I ask you a question, Mr. Hank?"

"Anything."

"Why are you staying? Brent said they gave his parents tons of money for their house."

"Wes, this place right here is all I have. Y'all are my family." Mr. Hank stretched his wrinkled brown hand in the direction of our house. "Your parents shook me out of that awful place I was in when Sheila went to glory. Besides, who'd keep you out of trouble if I leave?"

"But don't you want the money?"

"Money comes and goes, but family is forever."

I liked the realness of that.

We sat there watching the moving truck fill up with boxes. The only sound between Mr. Hank and me was the occasional teeth smack or a long, low "Hmmm." I knew Mr. Hank would never speak a bad word against a neighbor, but his frigid posture wasn't from the December air.

"When you gonna tell me about whatever y'all working on with that teacher from your school?" Mr. Hank asked.

My back tensed a little. "Ummmm" was the only thing that escaped my lips.

"Didn't say you had to tell me what it is. Just asked *when* you gonna tell me."

"Soon. Like in fourteen days soon," I answered.

Mr. Hank's silence was enough to say he understood.

31

It was two days before Christmas, and Mom, Dad, and I loaded into the SUV and drove to the Southside, where Mya lived. The drive to her house took about twenty minutes.

As we drove south, the houses got bigger and the yards grew farther apart. The Christmas decorations got better too. One house was lit up like Santa's workshop, complete with mechanical elves riding a train across the yard and music playing over a loudspeaker. Christmas decorations in the Oaks were simple; the best I'd seen were at Alyssa's house, with icicle lights draped around the front door. It was like a completely different city over here near Mya's.

We turned off the main road, entered Mya's neighborhood, and parked in the clubhouse's lot. Her neighborhood was fancy like that. No cars were allowed on the street.

As we walked up the long, curvy driveway to Mya's house, the lights from the decorations lit the entire yard and spilled out onto the street. The trees in front of the house were dripping in white lights, and the pillars flanking the front door were wrapped in red velvet ribbon, like candy canes. A small wreath hung from each window, dressed with red and gold bows. While we waited for someone to answer the doorbell, I counted eight of them.

Mrs. Cooper opened the door dressed in a long, silky silver dress. Her dark brown hair was cut into a short stacked style.

"Merry Christmas! Maxine, Walter, thank you for coming!" she said. "Wes, so good to see you." She grabbed me and pulled me in for a tight hug. She smelled sweet, like chocolate and toasted marshmallows.

"Thank you so much for inviting us," Mom said.

Mya peeked around the corner as we walked into the house. She wore a shorter version of her mom's dress. Her hair was pinned up into a knot, with one hanging curl that brushed her cheek.

"Hi, Wes, you look nice. Glad you came," she said. Her eyes were happy and shy.

"Thanks."

"Come in the kitchen. Alyssa, Brent, and Jas are already here."

I always have a hard time staying mad at Mya. She has a way of convincing me that she's right and I'm wrong. Even if she never says it.

I followed Mya through the museum-like front

room, big and gray-white, with a colossal Christmas tree.

In the kitchen, I found the crew standing next to a table loaded with fancy food. Staring back at me was a collection of silver domed platters, bowls of colorful fruit and vegetables, mini stuffed croissants, and shrimp wrapped with something that looked like thin bacon. The air was almost as tight as Brent's shirt.

"Wassup, Brent? I should've known you would be parked near the food," I said.

"Hey, Wes. Man, you have to try out this prosciutto-wrapped shrimp," Brent said, walking over to give me some dap.

"What do you know about prosciutto?" Jas teased.

"Nothing, until now!" Brent said, stuffing another shrimp into his mouth.

Alyssa was wearing a red dress with sequins all over it. I didn't ever remember seeing her in red before, but I liked it.

"Your dress is pretty," I said.

"It's new," she said. "And I love your vest."

"Thanks." I ran my hand over my new gray-and-black vest. I'd paired it with a crisp white shirt, a slim black tie, black jeans, and black-and-white Chucks. I knew I looked good. And from the way Alyssa was smiling at me, she knew it, too.

• • •

Mr. Cooper stared at us from across the room. He was fake-laughing with some white people who looked snobby enough to live in Mya's neighborhood. Mr. Cooper isn't what I would call a nice guy, but today he seemed extra *not* nice. I got the feeling he didn't like all these people in his house, stepping on his reflective tile floors, eating his extravagant food, and he especially didn't like us kids joking loudly around his guests.

As the kitchen started to fill with adults, we escaped to the media room with a platter of food. We passed another Christmas tree at the entrance of the media room. It was smaller than the last one but still way bigger than the tree crowded in our family room at home.

A massive sectional sofa took up one side of the media room; it was centered in front of a seventy-five-inch projector screen that served as the TV. Brent, Jas, Alyssa, Mya, and I collapsed on the sofa to watch. It was almost like old times in the Oaks—minus the enormous house. Minus the giant TV. Minus Kari.

"How's your new school?" Jas asked Mya.

"It's good. Most of my neighbors go there, so I already know a lot of people," Mya answered. "I miss you guys, though, and it's kinda weird being the only Black girl in most of my classes."

"You're Black?" Brent asked, pretending to be surprised.

"Shut up, Brent!" Mya yelled. She threw a grape at his head. He ducked just in time for it to miss him and land on the floor. We all laughed. Every single one of us missed the back-and-forth with Brent and Mya. "You know you're always teasing me for being too white, but the kids at my new school tease me for being too Black. Especially if I wear my hair in cornrows—and I can't even mention my old neighborhood without someone joking about how I survived the hood. I'm kinda over it."

"You want me to straighten somebody for you?" Brent asked.

"No, Brent! It's not that serious. . . . I just want to be me, without all the extra Black and white stuff," Mya said.

"Yeah, but it's not something you can turn on and off," Alyssa said.

"Why can't I just be Mya without being called Black or white?"

"The same reason none of us can erase our black skin," Brent said. "Or our brown skin, or Jas's light brownish skin—but you know what I mean."

"Yeah . . . ," Mya said. "I'm just tired of having to be two different people."

"You can be one Mya around us," Alyssa said, motioning with her arm to Brent, Jas, and me.

I kinda felt bad that Mya was dealing with this—I'd thought her new life was perfect this whole time. I guess not.

"But for real, though, I'll chill on the white jokes. And you figure out how to be Mya—the Black *and* white side of you," Brent said.

"Thanks, Brent. You guys really are my best friends, even Kari, when he's not doing something stupid," Mya said.

"You're our best friend too, Mya. Right, Wes?" Jas said, trying to get me to join the conversation.

"Yeah, you are . . . and you know you aren't too good to come back to the Grove, right?" I said. As soon as it slipped out, I regretted it. I knew Mya wouldn't let me get away with that dig. And she was trying to be nice.

"From what I hear, you may not be at the Grove much longer either," she said with a smirk. "My mom said lots of people have already moved out, and it's only a matter of time before everyone goes."

"We aren't going anywhere!" I said, but I only half believed it. Deep down I knew the odds of getting the historic designation were slim. And even if we *did* get designated, the Oaks would never be a complete puzzle again. Too many pieces were missing now.

32

Christmas break was over and it had been fifty-one days since we'd submitted the paperwork to the North Carolina State Historic Preservation Office—six whole days longer than it was supposed to take. Today was the day we'd find out if Kensington Oaks had been approved for the historic place designation. That afternoon, me, Mom, and Dad were going to the Save Our City office to find out the verdict. I had to keep calm until then.

Math block zipped by pretty quick. Ms. Hardy had chilled out a little and was giving me a little extra help when I needed it. *Math Jeopardy!* was a monthly thing now, and I was getting more answers right than wrong lately. Ms. Hardy still had her irky returning-quiz ritual, but these days I was safely in the so-so group, and last week I had even landed in the good group. I couldn't believe I was getting good at geometric calculations.

During lunch, I listened to Jas practice his drum solo in the band room. It had become the band's official opener, and Jas practiced it every chance he got. I closed my eyes and let the beat surround me. It vibrated through the walls, across the floor, up my legs, and into my chest. I'd heard it bunches of times now, but it never lost its power.

The afternoon crept by extra slow. Then, finally, the magic words crackled over the intercom:

"Wesley Henderson, please report to the front office for early dismissal."

It was time.

On the drive to the Save Our City office, I prayed over and over for good news. I wasn't sure if prayer actually worked, but it was worth a shot. Mom and Dad were pretty quiet too; maybe they were saying the same prayer.

"Come on in!" Ms. Monica greeted us when we arrived.

I was shocked at how plain the office was. I thought it would be on the fifteenth floor of one of those tall glass buildings downtown, with shiny windows and swanky furniture. Instead, it was in a small house in a regular neighborhood. The walls inside were covered with photographs of smiling children from all over the city—almost like Mr. Baker's classroom.

"These are all the families we've helped over the years. I hope we can add you and your neighbors to this wall," Ms. Monica said.

Even weirder was Mr. Baker standing beside Ms.

Monica in one of the photos—and they were holding hands. I think that rumor about Mr. Baker's wife was true . . . and he was always in the same places as Ms. Monica.

"Are you and Mr. Baker married?" I blurted out, not sure if she would even answer.

"Not yet," she said, winking at me. "But soon."

Kari had been right this whole time.

"Now, let's go. I have some news to share with you," Ms. Monica said.

"Good news?" I asked.

"Let's go find out."

Ms. Monica's office was just off the front room. I sat down on the couch beside Mom and Dad. I had jumping beans in my legs. I could barely sit still.

"I'll start with the good news," said Ms. Monica, beaming. "Kensington Oaks has been officially declared a nationally historic place. The designation extends to the ten blocks of homes, the community center, the park, and all walking areas."

For a moment Mom, Dad, and I just sat there stunned.

"For real?" I asked. Simmons was a big, powerful company, and after all this time, I'd been starting to think that that moral arc would never bend toward justice for the Oaks.

"Yes," Ms. Monica said, nodding.

"This is the best news I've gotten in years!" Mom said.

Dad sat quietly, but his shoulders relaxed and his eyes were suddenly brighter. "Thank you for all your hard work. You have no idea what this means to us," he said.

"This wouldn't have happened without Wesley and his stellar research," Ms. Monica said. "There are a lot of new members on the council, and none of them had heard of Mr. Pippin. We had a little history lesson when I showed them everything you uncovered."

"That's cool," I said.

"It is, but I do have some things I need to explain." Ms. Monica's voice went from sunny to partly cloudy in a matter of seconds.

I filled my lungs with clean air and prepared for the worst.

"The historic place designation won't stop gentrification from happening. Your neighbors will be able to sell their homes whenever they want, and you have no control over who moves in, but the designation will slow the process. For the houses that have been sold, any demolition will be halted for up to three hundred sixty-five days while design guidelines are developed."

"So, does that mean no condo building?" I asked.

"That's right," said Ms. Monica. "We'll push for

guidelines that restrict the size and design of any new construction. That means no large multifamily buildings. There will likely be changes happening in your neighborhood, but the changes will be less drastic with this designation in place."

"We can handle that," Mom said.

This felt like the changing point Mr. Baker was always talking about. It's true, change never stops, and we'd just changed things in a good way.

"If you need anything, please let me know. And congratulations!"

The rhythm from Jas's solo drumbeat replayed in my ears on the way home. The beat thumped through my body. Yeah, it was powerful, and for the first time in a long time I felt like I was too.

33

"I call this meeting to order at 6:01 p.m. We've got some important news to share with you, but I would first like to say thank you." Mom's smile lit up the dingy community center. "Thank you for showing up here tonight, and thank you for still being here, and a special thank-you to Monica Greene from Save Our City. I would like to call my persistent and sometimes stubborn son, Wesley, up here to join me."

I went up to stand with Mom at the front of the room. The crowd was so small compared to when we first started. I think people were tired of fighting.

My tongue swelled as I turned toward the audience. "Ahem, like my mom said . . . we have good news. The Oaks . . . I mean, Kensington Oaks is now a nationally historic place."

"What does that mean?" someone called from the crowd.

"Um, it means the condo building won't be built."

"What does that have to do with a historic district?" someone else called out.

Beads of sweat started to drip from my hairline. I shoved my hands behind my back.

"I think it protects us . . . ," I started, looking nervously at Mom. I was screwing this up.

Steam rose from my neck and flushed my face.

"Excuse me, I would like to invite Monica to answer any other questions you might have," Mom said, rescuing me.

Ms. Monica joined us at the front of the room.

"Hello. I have had the pleasure of working with the Hendersons to take back your block," Ms. Monica said. "The designation Wesley spoke of is very important, as it means any new construction or improvements to Kensington Oaks must adhere to guidelines established by the city."

"I still don't understand what all this means," Mrs. Silva called out.

Another voice came from the back of the room: "Me either!"

Mom and Ms. Monica took turns answering everyone's questions. Ms. Monica explained how the designation would protect us from Simmons and any other development company coming in and tearing down our homes to put up a huge condo building. That was a big deal!

After the meeting was over, I stayed with Mr. Hank to stack chairs. I didn't feel like going home yet.

"Wes, let me just say this," he said after everyone cleared out. "I am proud of you, young man. You helped make this happen. Some people won't get it, and that's okay. This was something worth fighting for, and you spoke up for all of us."

"Thanks," I said. I knew Mr. Hank was right, but I wanted everyone to be as happy as I was.

I walked outside to wait on Mr. Hank while he finished closing up the building. Before I could turn around, the scent of cocoa butter and vanilla tickled my nose.

There was Alyssa, wrapped in a lavender peacoat and matching scarf. Her cornrows were covered with a cream-and-purple-striped hat, and she rocked purple high-top Pumas.

"Hey, Alyssa," I said, my heartbeat speeding up.

"Hi, Wes," she said. "You did a great job up there. When did you become Mr. Save-the-Day?"

"I had to do something. My bad for not telling you about it."

"That's okay; this will be great for the Oaks."

"You really think so?"

"Yep! You weren't worried, were you?"

"Nope," I lied. "Can I walk you home?"

"Sure."

I stuck my head back inside the community center

to let Mr. Hank know I was leaving. I paused a second to coax my breath to a slower pace. *Drive slow, Wes.*

"Let's go," I said, turning to Alyssa.

I reached for her shivering hand. She wrapped her fingers around mine. I held on as tight as I could. We strolled through the neighborhood, under an arc of massive oak trees. As we walked hand in hand, the streets of the Oaks started to feel like home again.

34

The dreaded day had arrived.

It was finally time for me to deliver my presentation on social justice to my social studies class. Mr. Baker had agreed to wait until after we found out about the designation, and I couldn't put it off any longer. After I'd bombed at the community board meeting, I wasn't sure I could speak in front of an audience. I thought back to how cool Brent had been giving his presentation. If I could just have a little of his calm.

"Good afternoon, class. Wesley will be presenting his research on a very important social justice topic, so please give him your undivided attention." Mr. Baker's deep voice bounced off the walls.

I walked slowly to the front of the room and peered out at my classmates: fifty-four uninterested eyeballs gazed back at me. I didn't blame them; it had been weeks since we'd covered social justice. Mr. Baker had moved on to world geography. I found Alyssa on the second row—at least she seemed to be interested.

I stuffed my sweating palms into my pant pockets,

hoping no one would notice how nervous I was. *Think happy thoughts. Pretend you're in a room all by yourself.* I tried to replay all the advice I'd ever heard on public speaking. It didn't work—I was going to bomb. Again. And my feet hurt. Mom had convinced me to wear my Sunday shoes. Bad idea.

"Wesley, the floor is yours," Mr. Baker said.

"Ahem. Hey, everybody," my voice squeaked out.

"A little louder, Wesley," said Mr. Baker.

"Hey, everybody," I started again. "I chose gentrification as my social justice topic. If you're like I was, you have no idea what that is, right?"

"Right," the class answered.

"It's a little hard to explain, but I'll do my best." That got a couple smiles. And that made me relax a little. "Gentrification is when urban neighborhoods are renovated to appeal to upper-middle-class people. This usually means lower-income people are forced out or displaced. Kinda like what is happening around here."

That got everyone's attention. A few kids even leaned forward in their chairs.

"I started my research because I wanted to save my neighborhood, Kensington Oaks," I continued. I went on to explain the offer from Simmons Development Group and how I researched Kensington Oaks and found the history of Frederick Pippin.

"Mr. Pippin was the first Black man in our state to own and operate a lumber mill. He employed and helped lots of families."

I passed around newspaper articles and photographs of Pippin's Lumber Mill and Pippin Village. "The kids you see lived right on the land where I live today; that's the kind of history I wanted to protect."

Then I explained how Kensington Oaks received its historic place designation. It actually started to feel like I was just talking to them, not like I was giving a whole speech.

"I think Black people's history is important not just in February. It's also important that we use our voices to call out things that are wrong, like the city erasing Mr. Pippin's legacy.

"Earlier this year, when our neighborhood was having a block party, a white police officer stopped my friend Kari and took him to the police station for no reason at all. I kept thinking it was wrong, and I couldn't figure out why he did it. That officer wasn't from our neighborhood and didn't respect it. I may never know the exact reason he picked on Kari, but I do know our people and spaces deserve to be respected like everyone else's."

I looked out at everyone with their eyes fixed on me. Alyssa was giving me a silent handclap from her seat.

"I'm happy we were approved for the designation,

but I know that alone won't save Kensington Oaks, or other neighborhoods like it. The most important thing I learned is, we have to work together to protect our history and glow up our own neighborhoods. That's the only way to take back our blocks."

I'd gotten out everything I wanted to say without freezing up, and I felt unstoppable.

"That's all, thank you."

Brent jumped to his feet and started a round of applause. A wave of claps and cheers surrounded me. I stood at the front of the room, speechless. I had only hoped to get through my presentation without falling over. I didn't expect any of this.

"Wesley, I want to personally thank you for your hard work and impeccable research. Not only have you changed Kensington Oaks forever, you restored Mr. Pippin's legacy," Mr. Baker said. "Class, this is why I wanted you to research social justice. Being aware of what's happening in society connects us to the world around us. Wesley found a much deeper connection than I expected! And we can all learn something from his persistence."

As the class filed out of the room, Brent walked over to me. "You did it. Wasn't sure how this would all turn out, but I should've known you'd fix it. And you didn't even make it all about you," he said, poking me in the arm.

I laughed. I know Brent was joking, but he was right. It wasn't just about saving my house. It was about Mr. Pippin and Mr. Hank, Alyssa and her mom, the Silvas, and everyone else who loved the Oaks as much as I did.

I couldn't wait to tell Mom how great the presentation went. I swapped out my Sunday shoes for my Air Max 90s and ran the whole way home.

I had stopped at the entrance to our driveway to catch my breath when I noticed Mom's car wasn't parked in its normal spot. My parents never left me home alone. I didn't know what was up.

"Wes, come on over here," Mr. Hank called from across the street.

"Where's Mom?" I asked as soon as my breathing returned to normal.

"Something happened at Kari's school . . . another fight. The school kicked him out for good this time. Your parents went to help Tasha see what they could do about gettin' that boy out of trouble."

35

It was nearly midnight when Mom and Dad got home. I waited up watching reruns of *Black-ish* while Mr. Hank snored in the recliner. Before Dad could get the key into the door, I ran over and swung it open.

Kari stood behind Mom, staring at the ground. Even with his head down, I could see his bulging black eye. For the second time in one day, I was speechless.

"Thanks, Hank. We appreciate you looking after Wes," Mom said as Mr. Hank got up from his nap in the recliner.

"No problem at all. Y'all got that boy straight?" Mr. Hank asked the question like he didn't notice Kari was there. But I knew he noticed. . . . Mr. Hank notices everything. He walked toward the door and patted Kari on the back.

"That's a task for a new day," Dad said to himself as he locked the door behind Mr. Hank.

I didn't think Kari was mad at me, but we hadn't spoken since Thanksgiving, so I couldn't be sure. I stole another quick glance at his eye. It wasn't that bad . . . for a black eye.

Dad moved away from the door and turned to me. "Kari will be staying with us for a while. We need to set some ground rules, but we'll talk more about that in the morning."

All it took was Kari getting beat up again for my parents to see he needed to live with us. They should have listened to me the first time!

"Okay, guys, off to bed we go. Wes, you have school tomorrow. Grab a blanket and a pillow for Kari," Mom instructed. "Kari, you taking the couch or Wes's room?"

"Couch," Kari said. His voice sounded broken.

My stomach twisted. Kari always slept in my room when he stayed over.

I stacked a blanket and a pillow on the couch and wandered to my room.

I sprawled out across my bed and counted the beams on the ceiling from the streetlight shining outside my window. My brain sped in circles. *How long will Kari stay? Does Kari even want to live here now?* I wanted Kari here, but not like this.

I nodded off to sleep thinking about how fixing one thing ended up messing up something else.

I jerked awake when I heard footsteps in the hall. My door creaked open.

"Kari?" I asked.

"Yeah," he said.

"You good?"

"I don't know."

Kari stepped inside and lay across the bottom of my bed, his feet hanging off the edge.

"You mad at me?" I asked.

"Nah," Kari said. "I just feel like I didn't belong anywhere. Not in that apartment downtown, or that hotel, or at my aunt's."

That hit me hard. I'd never once doubted where I belonged—I've always had a home with Mom and Dad. I just wanted that same thing for Kari.

"You belong here," I said. "In the Oaks. We're a family. Glad you're back home."

EPILOGUE

I spent the morning of my twelfth birthday in summer heat carrying a sign that read TAKE BACK THE BLOCK.

A neighborhood on the east side of town was being torn apart. I was raising my voice to call out wrong things—I'd made sure to put on old sneakers, and I had gotten in some video game time the night before—so I didn't mind being there.

I spotted Brent walking across the construction site toward me; he'd grown at least an inch taller since the last time I'd seen him, and at least three inches over summer break.

"Brent, my man!" I called out. "Glad you came."

"Thanks for the invite. I'm your birthday present," Brent laughed, spreading his arms out wide. "So don't expect anything later."

Car horns beeped when the crowd spilled into the intersection in front of the construction site. I wasn't sure if the beeps were in dispute or support, but it didn't matter. The people of this neighborhood needed help. Brent, Kari, Jas, Alyssa, Mya, and I linked arms and stood in front of the construction site.

Yep, even Mya was there. I knew it was because Alyssa had begged her to come, but that was okay.

Mya and Kari had actually made up. I'd staged an intervention to get them cool again. Mya explained to Kari that it hurt her feelings when he didn't squash the rumor. She also agreed that she'd overreacted a bit. They hugged it out—clicking the last pieces of the puzzle into place, making the crew whole again.

■ ■ ■

Dad drove us back to my house to get cleaned up; then it'd be party time. I could hardly wait.

We'd spent the summer renovating the Oaks. After we got the historic place designation, the city donated twenty thousand dollars to make improvements to the neighborhood. We'd bought shiny new street signs, brighter bulbs for the streetlights, and a brand-new stone marker for the entrance of the neighborhood. We even had enough left over to get new rims and nets for the court.

I've turned into Mom—a much flyer version. I guess I do have that thing deep inside pushing me to seek out my own way. I am a leader.

Today was the unveiling of the renovated park; it was the perfect way to celebrate my birthday. The park was decked out with gold and white balloons and matching streamers. Flowers bloomed everywhere, all planted by Ms. Watkins. And best of all, the freshly bronzed water fountain shone from its new concrete pedestal.

DJ Jas's speaker blared above our heads while Brent and Alyssa got the crowd dancing—even Mr. Hank joined in. Mya danced through the crowd handing out fancy chocolate-covered ice cream bars, her birthday gift to me and a peace offering to the Oaks.

When Mom gave me the signal, I called everyone over to the fountain. "Welcome to the newly dedicated Frederick Pippin Village Park," I announced. "I'm happy to name this park after a man who deserves to have his legacy remembered. Mr. Pippin created a village here for families just like us; this space is part of our history, and I'm glad that future generations will enjoy it and remember him."

I stepped up to cut the bright red ribbon, welcoming all my neighbors—new and old—into the park. A tingle of pride sprinkled over me as I looked out at my community. Our community. Our family. Our home.

AUTHOR'S NOTE

Thank you for reading *Take Back the Block*!

While this story is loosely based on my hometown of Charlotte, North Carolina, my first up-close view and understanding of gentrification was during a visit to Harlem—a historic Black neighborhood in New York City that is known for its cultural richness and artistic expression. Nearly ten years ago, on a walking tour of Harlem, I quickly realized a change was happening, a change that would sweep a great amount of Black culture and history out of the city. I left that tour with the thought that gentrification was a big-city problem—until I returned home and faced the sad realization that the same sweeping of history was happening in my own town, just at a slower pace and on a smaller scale. Historic neighborhoods, parks, and restaurants would be there one month and gone the next. Beyond the places, what happened to the children and families? I wondered. That question plagued me for years and eventually became the motivation for *Take Back the Block*.

Frederick Pippin, his mill, and Pippin Village are

fictional, but there are many instances in American history of Black American inventors, artists, and business owners facing struggles similar to those depicted in my book. I wrote this story to shine a light on that reality and on the displacement of people living in urban communities, mostly spaces occupied by people of color.

Charlotte is experiencing an affordable-housing crisis brought on, in part, by rapid gentrification. As I discuss in this book, there is no easy fix. But don't be discouraged—there are things we can all do:

Speak up! Tell your story.

Join or donate to a local organization dedicated to preserving culture and history.

Write or call your local politicians to make sure they are advocating for marginalized people and spaces.

Share this book with your friends and family.

Thanks,
Chrystal

ACKNOWLEDGMENTS

Never in my biggest dreams did I imagine I would be here, sharing my words in this special moment. The praise for this divine place and path is due to my Savior.

There are some people who believed in the rough form of this book. Becky Shillington and Elizabeth Yahya, thank you for pushing me to continue down this road. Becky, all your predictions have come true so far; thank you for cheering me on and speaking up for me. Thank you, Skyler (Ari), for being my first young reader.

Many thanks to my critique group for your advice and listening ears.

I am proud to be affiliated with three powerful literary forces—We Need Diverse Books, DVPit, and Pitch-Wars. Because of these resources, I am blessed to have had two mentors along this journey: Gwendolyn Hooks and Maria Frazer. Thank you, Gwen, for so many encouraging words. Maria, you championed this book and taught me so much in such a short time—thank you.

My agent, Elizabeth Bewley at Sterling Lord Literistic, fell for my characters in a matter of hours. Elizabeth, your decisiveness in wanting to represent my work gave me so much confidence. Thank you for guiding me through this whirlwind and keeping my feet steady. Thank you, Danielle Bukowski and Szilvia Molnar at SLL, for working to share my book with the world.

My editor, Shana Corey at Random House Children's Books, first liked the pitch for this story through DVPit and loved it over a year later when it reached her in-box. Thank you, Shana, for helping me transform this ambitious collection of scenes into a book I am proud to have my name on. You validated my point of view and my characters and didn't shy away from the cultural aspects of this book. You pushed me to be better.

Thank you to the whole team at RHCB: Polo Orozco, Kathleen Dunn Grigo, Noreen Herits, Dominique Cimina, Barbara Bakowski, Alison Kolani, Barbara Perris, Christine Ma, Janet Foley, Adrienne Waintraub, Erica Stone, Kristin Schulz, Natalie Capogrossi, Shaughnessy Miller, Emily DuVal, John Adamo, Kelly McGauley, and Michelle Nagler. A special thank-you to Sylvia Al-Mateen for your sensitivity notes.

My sincerest gratitude to Michelle Cunningham for designing the cover and to the awesomely talented Richie Pope for the cover art—you brought Wes to life in such a special way.

A sincere thank-you to my fellow Black authors:

so many of you inspired me or freely gave advice or encouragement. I am proud to be a part of this movement with you.

I would not have been able to navigate these waters without my therapist. Thank you for helping me find peace.

I come from a family of incredibly strong women. My grandmother Henrietta is the strongest woman I know—I hope I've made you proud. I love you, Gram.

My mother, Doris, taught me the power of speaking up and speaking out. Mom, you've fought so many battles for so many—thank you for your example.

To my siblings, a warm thank-you to LaShanda and Roddrick: you both exude tenacity and a never-give-up spirit. I love you. Trinisha, you always push me to try new things and conquer my fears. Your persistence is changing the world; keep kicking down doors.

Ezra, my son, my heart, my sweet baby. Everything I thought I knew about myself changed when I looked into your eyes. You inspire me to live life more deeply. I love you.

I am blessed to have a husband who is also my best friend. Jeremy, you believed in me way before I believed in myself. Thank you for being my partner in life and along this journey.

To all aspiring authors: keep writing—your voices and stories matter.

ABOUT THE AUTHOR

Chrystal D. Giles is making her middle-grade debut with *Take Back the Block*. Chrystal was a 2018 We Need Diverse Books mentee, and her poem "Dimples" appears in the poetry anthology *Thanku: Poems of Gratitude* (Millbrook). Chrystal lives in Charlotte, North Carolina, with her husband and son.

chrystaldgiles.com
@creativelychrys